How much more did she need to know?

"Greg, I have a million questions."

"We'll get to your questions…later," he promised. His voice threaded through the blackness, entwining them in intimacy. Gently he pulled her toward him.

"But—"

"Hush." His hand brushed her cheek, drawing her mouth closer to his. "Your skin is so soft, 'Kella," Greg murmured against her lips. "Soft." He nipped the lower lip ever so lightly. "Sweet." And then his lips were there, demanding a response she was anxious to give.

McKella moaned, twisting slightly in an effort to get closer. Her hands roamed over his back, and her breasts pressed against the thin material that separated her from the hard wall of his chest. "What are you doing to me?" she whispered when his lips drew back. "Who are you, really?"

"You know me." His words hung in the darkness. "I'm the man who's falling in love with you."

Dear Reader,

Thirty-one years ago this month, my husband and I flew to the island of Bermuda for our honeymoon. We've never forgotten the beauty of the island, the friendliness of the people or the incredible blue shades of the water and the sky.

The rescue scene on the beach actually happened much as I depicted. It was the first and only time I've ever been part of a human chain in a rescue situation. Very scary, but with a thankfully happy ending.

After all these years, Bermuda has changed greatly, so I took some minor liberties in my story. As far as I know, there are no outdoor cafés in St. George like I describe. Nor do the honeymoon cottages exist, though I understand there is something similar nearby.

Still, when I think of a honeymoon, I think of Bermuda. The island holds a magical appeal for me that made it the perfect setting for this story. I hope you'll agree.

Happy Reading!

Dani Sinclair

Married in Haste
Dani Sinclair

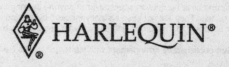

TORONTO • NEW YORK • LONDON
AMSTERDAM • PARIS • SYDNEY • HAMBURG
STOCKHOLM • ATHENS • TOKYO • MILAN • MADRID
PRAGUE • WARSAW • BUDAPEST • AUCKLAND

For Mary and John LaFond, whose precious gift of friendship
has spanned more than twenty-four years of wonderful
memories so far. Also for Natashya Wilson. Your enthusiasm
for this story meant a great deal. And always, for Roger, Chip,
Dan and Barbara.

Special thanks to Don Black who was willing to share his
piloting knowledge with a stranger.

ISBN 0-373-22481-8

MARRIED IN HASTE

Copyright © 1998 by Patricia A. Gagne

Printed in U.S.A.

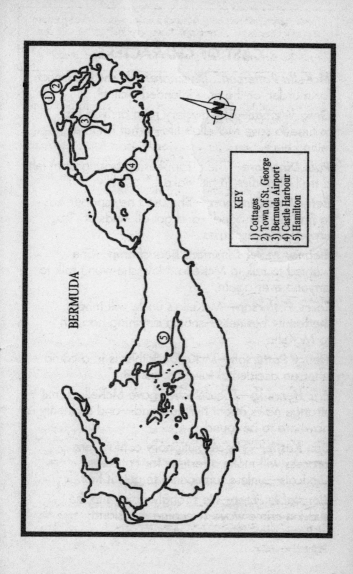

BERMUDA

KEY
1) Cottages
2) Town of St. George
3) Bermuda Airport
4) Castle Harbour
5) Hamilton

CAST OF CHARACTERS

McKella Patterson...Dinsmore?—Is she a suspect for murder, or the next intended victim?

Greg Wyman—The mystery man arrived just in time to save McKella's life—what isn't he telling her?

Paul Dinsmore—The disappearing bridegroom left a trail of bodies in his wake.

Betty Jane Dinsmore—She used newspaper ads to find her husband—and got all kinds of unwelcome responses.

Eleanor Miller Dinsmore Beauchamp—She wanted to talk to McKella. Now she won't talk to anyone ever again.

Larry Patterson—McKella's uncle will inherit the family business—should anything happen to McKella.

Henry Patterson—McKella's father is in a coma after an accidental fall—or was it?

Eric Henning—The detective gave McKella some strange news about her husband—and suddenly is nowhere to be found.

Ben Kestler—His revolutionary contact lens process will make a fortune for Patterson Opticals—unless someone else gets it first.

Constable Freer—He strongly objects to the sudden crime wave sweeping the island of Bermuda.

Prologue

The stench of his own sweaty fear assaulted his nostrils. His breathing made a harsh raspy sound even in the noisy bar. It had taken surprising courage to approach the man after the other people had left. Especially since he wasn't sure he wanted to hear the answer to his question spoken out loud. Didn't he already know the answer in his heart?

The badly scarred table sat between them. He fingered his glass of beer. This was more difficult than he'd anticipated, but he'd walked and hitchhiked for the past two days. He wasn't about to let a scowl chase him off.

Slowly, he withdrew the battered cloth wallet from his coat pocket and laid it on the table. His body tightened in anticipation as those blue eyes looked from the wallet to his face.

"How did you find me?"

He sensed fear behind that question. The fear surprised him, so his shrug was quick. "I asked some questions. The trial made the local papers, you know.

When I found your wallet in my brother's dresser, I thought you might want it back.''

"Yeah? Why are you really here?"

"I want the truth about my father," he stated quietly.

His companion's lips drew back in a snarl of anger that distorted the handsome face so strangely like his own.

"Go home."

"I don't have a home anymore." His voice deepened, betraying the need behind his question. "Who killed my father?"

Weary eyes closed for a moment, then opened. "You're crazy. He fell into Miller's pond and drowned."

His fist smashed against the tabletop, sending the beer sloshing onto the dirty wood surface and startling both of them. The beers he'd already drunk had begun to make him feel light-headed. He wasn't used to drinking.

"They fought earlier that night," he said, striving for better control.

Resignation replaced surprise on the face across from him. "So what? They always fought. Your father was a drunk. A child abuser."

That single truth serrated him with white hot pain. Memory of all the wicked beatings stirred his anger. But he held it in check, noting the other man hadn't questioned who "they" were.

"The sheriff wrote Pop's death up as an accident."

There was no softening of the features staring so intently at him. A lock of the other man's black hair fell forward to cover his forehead. He pushed at his own dark hair with a hand that still wasn't steady.

"Leave it alone. It's over. There's nothing you can do. Your father's dead."

"The sheriff thinks you killed him."

Fury lit his companion's features. "Me? Or your brother?"

"Either of you. Both of you. You're the one with the temper."

Blood drained from those features. Both hands became fists.

"*I* can prove where I was that night."

"With Eleanor?"

"Shut up."

"Guess who she's been dating since you left? Think she'd give both of you an alibi?"

He watched as his companion reached for his beer and drained the glass, setting it back down with careful precision. The man's hand was rock steady, but his expression looked hunted. What was he afraid of?

"I don't have any answers for you." The man's chair scraped the floor as he stood abruptly and swayed. His words were just the tiniest bit slurred. "Go back to Tweaksburg."

"Hey, wait! You can't just leave."

"Watch me."

He pushed back his own chair in panic, but the intensity of that gaze kept him in his seat. "Take me with you."

The words hung in the smoker's haze that surrounded them.

"You can get to hell without my help. There're people looking for me. If *you* found me, they won't be far behind. You're smart. You've got a future…"

"I've got nothing," he argued. "You think a fancy

grade-point average is going to make me somebody? Not likely. Take me with you."

"No." The man turned and walked away.

He scrambled to his feet and watched in helpless dread as the hot, summer night swallowed the closest thing he'd ever had to a friend.

It took a moment for him to notice the wallet, still sitting open on the table. Part of it lay in a puddle of beer. He knew there was no money or credit card inside, but there was a driver's license and a social security card—and a picture of Eleanor.

He picked up the wallet and studied the picture. He, too, wanted good things. Rich things. Things he couldn't have back in Tweaksburg, Kentucky. Did it really matter how his father had died? Hadn't he been sure of the truth before he even came searching for answers?

He drained his glass and followed the other man out the door. The beers had gone straight to his head, but they'd also given him courage. He wasn't going back to Tweaksburg. If his old friend wouldn't take him along, he'd demand a ride as far as the next town. After all, he had nothing to go home to.

Drunk or not, his father hadn't drowned in Miller's pond without help.

Chapter One

"Repeat after me. I, McKella Patterson, take you, Paul Dinsmore…"

She stared at Paul's too-handsome face through the veil of her gown and felt a sudden chill. Yet, this was the right thing to do. She'd thought it all out so carefully.

Love was a fantasy. This was reality.

"McKella?"

Her eyes flicked to the minister, a friend of her father's for many years. Her father sat in the front pew behind them, dying by the minute. He wanted this union with every breath he took.

She wanted it, too.

Didn't she?

Of course she did. This was the right thing to do.

"I, McKella Patterson, take you…"

Satisfaction gleamed in Paul's blue eyes. The heavy weight in her stomach didn't lessen. For just a moment, she thought she'd be ill.

DANCERS SWIRLED AROUND HER, but McKella felt blessedly isolated. The reception was running without a hitch, even if her grin was etched in place. She wished desperately that she could leave this crowded, noisy room.

"There you are, my dear." Her uncle appeared at her side. Larry Patterson was an aggressively lean, fit man in his early fifties and her father's only other living relative. "I got your father back to the house. He's completely exhausted, but the nurse is there."

She gave him a weak smile. "I'm anxious to be away, too," she told him honestly.

"Your groom doesn't seem to be in any hurry."

Her gaze followed his across the room to where Paul danced with a slender, attractive brunette whose casual clothing seemed terribly out of place at this fancy reception. The woman didn't look to be having a lot of fun, either. Her features were grim as she listened to something Paul said.

"McKella! Shouldn't you be thinking about changing?"

McKella turned to face her maid of honor, but her stomach muscles tightened and she couldn't respond. Why was she feeling so apprehensive?

"I'll let Paul know you went to the suite," her uncle promised with a smile.

McKella turned back in Paul's direction, only to find both he and the woman had disappeared. Her gaze landed instead on a man leaning negligently against the far doorway. An inexplicable tension gripped her. His dark curly hair reminded her of Paul's, but there was a raw energy about this man, as though his lazy pose was just that.

She wished that her contact lens hadn't ripped that morning. Or that she at least had her glasses with her. She couldn't make out his features, and for some reason she wanted a clear view of this man. The irony didn't escape her. She, the new owner of Patterson Opticals, didn't have a spare pair of contacts with her.

The stranger stared in her direction, head tipped slightly to one side. Dressed in dark slacks and a casual shirt open at the collar, he obviously wasn't one of the two hundred fifty invited guests. There was something sensual, almost predatory in the way he stood there. Her breath seemed to catch in her throat.

Disturbed, she nodded in the direction of the stranger. "Who's that man?"

"What man?" her uncle asked.

Even as she would have pointed him out, the stranger took a step back through the doorway and was gone.

"What man, honey?"

Her maid of honor took her arm. "Come on, McKella. I'll help you get out of that dress."

"Never mind," McKella said, "he's gone." And she let her friend lead her away.

HALF AN HOUR LATER, McKella was reaching up to unfasten the small crystal-and-pearl earrings, when her maid of honor entered, her round face lined with concern.

"What's wrong?"

"It's Paul. Oh, McKella, he's drunk."

"What are you talking about?"

"Your uncle Larry is bringing him to the room, but Paul is really drunk."

"Not a chance." Paul was a social drinker. He could nurse a beer all evening. Tonight, as far as she knew, he'd only had two beers and some wine for the toasts. A shiver traced its way up her spine as she watched Paul and her uncle stagger into the room.

Paul could barely hold his head erect.

An hour later, he lay sprawled on the bed, his tuxedo jacket bunched across his back and under his armpits. His tie dangled in a loose knot beneath the open buttons on his shirt. His handsome face lay in repose, looking childishly innocent despite the gut-wrenching heaving of a few minutes earlier.

McKella knew Paul could not be drunk, even if he did display most of the symptoms. More than likely, he was coming down with the flu or something, and the alcohol had simply reacted more strongly than usual. She looked up and met her own worried expression in the mirror across the room.

Paul had fought her when she'd tried to remove his clothing. His refusal to call a doctor had left her feeling oddly intimidated. McKella wasn't used to being intimidated. She could hold her own in a board meeting filled with aggressive men. Why, then, couldn't she handle the man who was now her husband?

McKella walked to the other side of the bed and lifted the telephone, then hesitated. Paul had furiously insisted that he only needed sleep—and now he did look a little better. She rubbed her upper arm where his fingers had bitten into her skin. Maybe he was right. Maybe a doctor wasn't needed.

The dial tone hummed from the receiver in her hands. Automatically, her fingers tapped out the number for her townhouse. She hadn't checked her messages in three days. At least this would give her something to *do* on her wedding night.

She listened to two well-wishers before the automated voice alerted her that she also had a deleted message.

The telephone company's answering service held deleted messages for twenty-four hours before erasing them. This had proved a blessing once before when she'd deleted a message by mistake and then needed the person's phone number.

But she hadn't deleted any messages in the last twenty-four hours.

With a sense of foreboding, she depressed the numbers that would let her listen to the replay.

"McKella, this is Eric Henning again. I've tried to reach you several times and since you haven't returned my calls I may be too late, but you should definitely postpone your wedding."

A cold wash of fear flooded her insides as she looked down at her groom.

Eric Henning was a private investigator she'd hired before the wedding to run a background check on Paul. His investigation had turned up nothing unexpected.

"I was talking to some people in Lexington on another matter completely when Paul Dinsmore's name came up," the voice continued in her ear. "As a result of that conversation, I did a little probing. I think you'll be willing to pay some additional expenses when I tell you that not one of his references has ever met the guy."

"*What?*"

The recorded message droned on. "On paper, and even in their computer files, Paul Dinsmore exists. Only, it looks like he never worked for the Zuckerman Company. There are lots of possible explanations, but you ought to let me explore this further."

Eric had never been satisfied with his initial background check on Paul. When the strapping detective first suggested she postpone the wedding until he delved a little deeper, she'd disagreed, knowing her father's time was limited. Her father trusted Paul enough to groom him as the next CEO. More than that, he *liked* Paul. *She* liked Paul. A quick marriage had seemed like the right thing to do.

"Something is fishy here," Eric's voice persisted. "There are lots of possible explanations, but you ought to postpone your wedding until we can get at the facts."

"Now you tell me." Regret tasted bitter in her mouth. If she had waited even an hour longer to check her machine, she never would have known this message existed. And only one other person had her telephone codes.

Paul.

Anxiety squeezed the air from her lungs. She looked away from her sleeping husband to stare at the generic print hanging on the wall over the bed.

"This has to be a mistake."

She punched in the number Eric had left for her, but the phone rang, unanswered. She tried his office number, which rolled over to his answering service. As she stared at the stranger who was now her husband, she left an urgent message for Eric to call her at the hotel immediately.

PAUL HALTED IN THE MIDDLE of the crowded Bermuda terminal just outside customs. "McKella, sweetheart, I told you it's a misunderstanding. When your detective calls back, you'll find out he made a mistake."

She watched Paul submerge his anger in favor of the sexy persuasiveness that was such a deliberate part of him.

"Then why couldn't we have waited for him to explain?" she asked with a calm she was far from feeling.

"*I* explained! He made a mistake—or someone is playing a very unfunny practical joke." His icy blue eyes sent a chill racing up her forearms.

She wanted to believe Paul. She *did* believe him. There had to be a reasonable explanation. She mustn't give in to these crazy doubts that Eric's message had planted.

He rested his long tapered fingers along her suit jacket. "McKella, where is this lack of faith coming from? What have I ever done to deserve being investigated in the first place?"

The question wasn't as riveting as the glimpse she caught of something repellent hidden behind his affable exterior of amazing good looks and polished charm.

He could sell snake oil to a snake. Her father had said that about Paul from the beginning. Only, her father had meant the words to be complimentary.

"You married a businesswoman, Paul. I always check things out. We should have delayed our trip until we talked to Eric."

His grip tightened just a fraction. Then he broke off to rub at the bridge of his nose. Remorse stabbed her. She knew he had a terrible headache. He'd been downing aspirin tablets all day—when he wasn't dozing in an effort to overcome the effects of last night.

"You couldn't even reach the man for confirmation, McKella. It may have been someone else on the phone pretending to be him."

"It wasn't." She was certain of that.

"Are we supposed to miss our honeymoon over some hoax?" His angry eyes fastened on her. "Because that's what it is, McKella, a hoax. On Monday, you can call Zuckerman yourself. I'll give you the telephone number for the president's direct line."

"Then why did you erase Eric's message?"

His laugh was bitter. "Look at you. Look at what you're thinking right now. Of course I erased that damn message. It was obviously a prank—somebody's idea of a sick joke. Or else it was a scam and that clown was planning to hit you up for more money."

Uncertainty made her waver. Eric wouldn't scam her, but he could have been misled.

"Look, McKella, I wish you had come to me with your doubts."

"I don't—"

"Obviously, I did something to make you doubt me this way." Regret and pain etched lines around his mouth. "We probably shouldn't have rushed the wedding, but I thought it was what you wanted, considering your father's condition. Maybe I expect too much to think you should trust *my* word over that of some sleazy PI."

"I do tr—"

"I didn't want to hang around this morning and miss our plane waiting for that clown to call back and tell you it was a joke," he continued forcefully. "There are two tropical depressions off the coast right now. I wanted to reach the island before flying became dangerous or prohibited. What if one of the storms decides to move or turn into a hurricane?"

"You *want* to be here during a hurricane?" Once more she tried for humor in an effort to diffuse his anger.

He didn't smile. If anything, his expression hardened. "*You* were most insistent that we honeymoon here."

The thinly veiled accusation stung. "You asked me where I wanted to go—"

"McKella, for God's sake, my head is splitting. I don't want to quibble with you over every little thing I say."

An older couple moved past them, luggage in tow. They eyed McKella and Paul with curiosity. McKella sent a quick glance around and realized that several people were watching them.

"You're right. The middle of the airport is hardly the place for this discussion."

"I'll get us a cab and we'll go to the resort."

He reached a hand toward her, but she stepped back out of range. She felt oddly detached and uncertain. This was not the affable man she had come to know. "You go ahead." The words came out before she could think.

He masked his anger so well no one would believe it existed. "Now I've made you angry. I'm sorry, darling. I know I'm not handling this well, but I have the grandfather of all headaches. I really don't want to fight with you."

He brushed back a coil of dark black hair that had fallen across his forehead, and she thought again that he was an extraordinarily handsome man.

"I was a jerk last night, getting sick and passing out like that. And I've been a jerk all day, sleeping when we should have been talking. Please forgive me. I'm annoyed, but not with you. I can prove your detective is lying easily enough."

Could he? McKella's stomach churned. Anyone else hearing Paul would be moved by such a heartfelt appeal.

Why wasn't she?

Paul's explanation was so plausible.

Only, Eric had an impeccable reputation. Patterson

had used his services for years. She *trusted* the detective.

Did that mean she didn't trust her husband?

McKella brushed aside the traitorous thought. Eric *could* have made a mistake. He was probably even now enroute to see Zuckerman to make certain of his facts. That would explain why he hadn't returned her calls. Still, she had to talk to the detective before she suffocated on the turmoil of her churning thoughts.

Paul was right about one thing: They'd rushed the wedding. She'd let her own wants, and her father's illness, influence her actions.

"Why don't you go on to the resort," she suggested as lightly as she could. She felt an overwhelming need to get away from Paul and to think this through. "I need to pick up a few things in town."

"McKella, we need to talk."

"I believe those were my words this morning." She tried to keep her emotions at bay but the constriction in her chest tightened further, heightening her need to escape. "Talking doesn't seem to be getting us anywhere at the moment."

Again, restrained fury danced beneath the surface of Paul's elegant facade. "That's because you aren't listening to me."

"Really? We're here, aren't we? I wanted to wait until we cleared this up, remember?"

Why had she never seen this implacable hardness in him before? Because she hadn't been looking. Because they'd never been at loggerheads over anything important before.

"I'm sorry, Paul," she continued more firmly, striving for at least an outward show of control. "I have a headache, too. We both need some space right now."

His eyes seemed to bore right through her.

She considered the man she thought she knew. Besides being strikingly handsome, Paul was well-spoken, with the leadership qualities and the experience necessary to take over the company she didn't want to run, that her uncle wasn't capable of running. Paul could also give her the family she craved, and at age thirty-two that had become an important issue for her.

She wasn't deluding herself. She knew their marriage was no love match—more of a *like* match. And she'd been willing to settle for that. It had seemed like the right thing to do.

Until last night.

Until Eric made Paul Dinsmore an unknown quantity.

"This is not how I wanted to start our honeymoon," Paul pressed. He tried for one of his more charming grins. "So far, I've been a dismal failure as a husband."

McKella couldn't return his smile nor dispute his words. "Give me a little time to—"

"One hour," he told her abruptly. "If you don't come to the cottage in one hour, I'll come get you." He didn't try to hide the threat, though he covered it with a smile that didn't reach his eyes.

"Really?"

He flinched at her response. At least he knew her well enough to read the steel beneath her soft tone.

"McKella, I didn't mean that to sound so—"

"Arrogant? Domineering?"

"McKella—"

"One hour," she agreed and turned on her spindly high heels so he wouldn't see the lie. For one wild moment, part of her expected him to grab her from behind—but of course he didn't. She stumbled and almost fell over her suitcase, ruining her exit. His strong hands steadied her, sending an unexpected jolt of distaste through her system.

Her handbag slipped from her fingers and clattered to the tile floor, raining debris. Paul bent to retrieve the scattered items, while she righted the suitcase and refastened the snap that had come undone. She chased after her sunglasses that had skittered across the tile floor, put them on, and accepted her purse without a word.

"Remember one thing," he said softly, "you're my wife now."

She curbed her instant, angry response, but his words echoed in her head as her heels snapped out a staccato rhythm toward the exit. She didn't have to look back to know that he watched her go.

Heat and humidity washed over her as soon as she stepped outside. Her suit melded to her skin and her carefully restrained hair dampened and clung to her scalp in its tight bun. The island was a sauna.

Wasn't there a song about how the Bermuda Triangle made people disappear? She fumbled with her large handbag, finding it open. If only the Bermuda Triangle could make her questions disappear. Had she been stupid just now? Had Eric been conned? Was she risking the end of her marriage over a prank or a scam?

Inside her bag, the coin purse had jostled its way to the top. Without delving any further, she pulled it out, knowing there was enough cash inside for a taxi ride.

The taxi driver took her into downtown St. George, close to the resort. She drew quite a few stares as she strolled down the busy sidewalk dressed in a cream-colored linen suit and teal-blue blouse. *Definitely the most overdressed woman on the island of Bermuda,* she thought. Even the policemen wore shorts.

She strolled past the shops and crowds of tourists, trying to push anger aside and put her thoughts in order. She needed to call Eric Henning again. The number he'd left had continued to ring unanswered this morning. Why hadn't he returned her messages?

Unless Paul was right about the call being a prank.

McKella made her way to a tiny outdoor café and, with a sigh, sank into an empty seat at a table near the sidewalk. The waiter was a delightful Bermudian who, undefeated by her choice of iced tea over the fruited rum drink, convinced her in his lilting dialect to try the house sandwich instead of a simple salad. McKella finally agreed, reminded of the same friendly pressure tactics her father and Paul had used to convince her to get married in the first place. She hadn't needed much persuasion then, either.

"When did I turn into such a wuss?"

A man sat down at the next table, drawing her gaze. He smiled sympathetically. "Don't feel bad," he told her. "He's very persuasive."

The stranger had a warm smile, McKella decided. She returned it, but quickly turned away, disturbed by her inner reaction to the man. He reminded her of Paul. Uneasily, she realized he also resembled the stranger lurking at her wedding yesterday. This couldn't be the same man, of course.

Still, her breathing quickened. If nothing else, this stranger was much too potently masculine for comfort. The last thing she needed was to get picked up by a sexy stranger on the prowl while she struggled with a conflict that might end her marriage twenty-four hours after the ceremony.

She asked the passing waiter about a telephone, intending to try Eric's number again, but a woman was already using the only pay phone and a man waited impatiently behind her.

McKella became conscious of the stranger watching her with frank approval. He lowered his head to a guide book, but she sensed his awareness of her every movement.

His dark curly hair and similar build were what reminded her of Paul, she concluded. They really didn't look alike up close. This man's features were more rugged, less perfect. When he glanced up and caught her staring, she averted her eyes and looked toward the street.

A group of moped bikers putted their way through the busy traffic, briefly forgetting to stay to the left as they turned the corner. The natives were used to tourists. Horns blared and the oncoming taxi missed the nearest biker, who quickly returned to her own lane.

McKella shook her head as the beaming waiter deposited an enormous croissant sandwich on her table. She ate mechanically, but the food soon restored her frazzled nerves, helping her to put things in perspective.

She shouldn't have allowed Paul's strange behavior to anger her. Her attempts to force a discussion over breakfast that morning had been met with a wall of stony silence, except for his insistence that they not miss their plane. He'd looked so ill that she'd allowed him to get away with his behavior. A mistake, she decided.

It would take them time to feel their way through the sudden changes in their relationship. Paul needed to understand that, while she was the boss at Patterson Opticals, at home she was his partner.

Leaving him at the airport had been another mistake. They were married. Frank discussion was essential if their marriage was going to work.

"No, it's still a tropical storm," the waiter assured the attractive man at the next table. "They say it may be a hurricane by morning, but don't worry, hurricanes seldom bother Bermuda."

"Actually," the man said in his low, pleasing baritone, "I wasn't worried about the island. I was more concerned that it would shut down the airport."

"That could be a problem," the waiter agreed.

McKella pushed aside the remainder of her sandwich. She would try to call Eric again, she decided. Then she would go to the cottage and talk with Paul.

Her fingers froze when she opened her purse and began to rummage for her wallet. Immediately, she realized the white envelope containing her birth certificate and the return plane ticket was gone.

Had she dropped it in the taxi?

No. She hadn't spilled a thing in the cab. The envelope must have fallen out at the airport when she'd dropped her bag. Paul had picked up everything except her glasses. She was certain nothing else had remained on the tile floor.

Heart pounding, she let the implication sink in. Had Paul kept the envelope? It was the only explanation.

"Is something wrong?"

The stranger gazed at her in concern. His brightly colored eyes were warm and caring. McKella straightened and tried for a polite smile. "Nothing. Thank you."

He didn't accept her delicate brush-off. His low

voice rumbled soothingly. "Have you lost your wallet?"

Wallet.

She pushed her sunglasses to the top of her head, flipped open the purse, and once more shuffled the contents. Her change purse was there, but no matter how many times she moved things around, her change purse was there but her wallet—containing her identification, credit cards and checkbook—was gone.

"I'll be happy to pay for your meal. Do you think you might have left it in your hotel room?"

She stared at the man's rugged face without really seeing him, while the undigested sandwich rolled in her stomach. "I haven't been to the resort yet."

He pulled two bills from his wallet and handed them to her.

"What's this?"

"Some cash until you find your wallet."

When McKella tried to hand it back, her fingers brushed his hand, making them tingle in awareness. "No. Thank you."

"It's okay. Consider it a loan."

"I'm sure I have enough money to cover lunch."

He handed her a business card. "Greg Wyman."

She accepted the card without glancing at it. Despite the heat and humidity, she was cold, terribly cold. Paul had removed all her identification from her purse.

"Thank you, Mr. Wyman, but—"

"Greg."

"Greg." She didn't return his smile. "I really don't need—"

His head jerked up, staring past her as a car horn squawked loudly. Other horns followed suite. Someone shouted.

She'd grown used to the traffic noises and the roar of the incessant mopeds, but when she saw Greg's expression, McKella twisted to look behind her. A small truck weaved down the road, coming much too fast. Suddenly it veered toward the café scattering pedestrians, leaving bikers and cars hopelessly snarled.

A woman approached along the sidewalk, not paying the least bit of attention. She looked right at McKella as the truck struck her from behind.

Strong arms grabbed McKella. Greg yanked her from her seat and flung them both to one side. He buried her body beneath his own. The truck splintered through the low picket fence into the table where she'd been sitting, crushing it and Greg's against the café wall and shattering the plate-glass storefront of the pale-pink building.

The din was incredible. Voices shouted.

"Are you okay?"

McKella stared up into Greg's captivating blue-green eyes. "Thanks to you." Her voice sounded as breathless as she felt.

He rose and tugged her to her feet, then let her go and spun toward the wreckage. The woman's body lay on the sidewalk, bent at an impossible angle. Blood pooled in dark patches around her broken form. Her eyes, glazed in death, stared up at the china-blue sky.

Someone was screaming. A high penetrating sound that tore at the nerves. More voices shouted. People milled everywhere.

GREG DECIDED MCKELLA was in a mild state of shock, but otherwise all right. He moved to assist an older couple. It was too late to chase after the driver who'd leaped from the van, so he did what he could for the injured. He noticed McKella assisting the waiter, who had blood streaming from a cut on his forehead. Her wide brown eyes stood out against her pale face.

A policeman tapped him on the shoulder, and the questions began. Right now, giving the officer an accurate description of what had happened was more important than going to McKella. Still, Greg never lost sight of her—not even when she sat down after waving off help for her own injuries.

Her cream-colored suit was stained beyond redemption and the heel on one of her pumps had snapped off. Greg could see she'd scraped her knee, ruining her hose. And she kept rubbing her elbow as though it hurt.

Greg followed the policeman when he moved to question her. "You are all right, miss?" the policeman asked in his lilting voice.

"Yes, thanks to Mr. Wyman."

"Your name?"

"McKella Patterson."

As the policeman made more notes in his small book, she gave him her home address and the name of the resort she was staying at.

She'd given her maiden name by mistake, Greg realized, or else she'd kept her own name. She was, after all, a successful businesswoman.

But she wasn't much of a witness. She didn't seem to realize that this hadn't been an accident.

"I saw the truck strike that poor woman," she told the policeman. "Then Mr. Wyman threw me down out of the way. I'm afraid that's all I can tell you."

"Did you see the driver?"

"No. It happened too fast. Did his brakes fail?"

The policeman gave a shrug and moved on to the waiter.

"What happened?" she asked Greg.

"The driver took off."

"Took off?"

"He aimed the truck, floored the engine and jumped."

"What?" Horror made the word a bare whisper.

"He ran down the street." Greg waved his hand to indicate the direction. "A passerby gave chase, but the driver got away."

"You actually saw all this?"

"Only the truck heading for us and the man jumping out. I was facing that direction, don't forget."

"You saw him? The driver?"

Greg shook his head. "Not so I could recognize him. He was dressed in black with something covering his face."

"That should make him easy to find. I don't think they allow black clothing on the island."

He couldn't force a smile at her weak attempt at humor.

"This wasn't an accident."

McKella shuddered. "Of course it was. You don't think the driver was *trying* to kill that poor woman?"

"Or you. Or me."

Her mouth opened in shock. "What are you saying?" she whispered.

"We were the three people in his path—a path he deliberately chose. At a guess, I'd say he was aiming for the woman coming to talk with you."

"She wasn't coming to talk to me! I don't even know that woman."

But Greg did. At least, he thought he did. It had been years since he'd last seen her, but she hadn't changed that much.

McKella twisted toward the broken form on the concrete several feet away. Someone had covered the body with a tablecloth. McKella shuddered.

"I was probably the last thing that poor woman saw," she whispered.

Greg wanted to draw her into his arms and offer comfort. Instead he repeated, "She appeared to be coming over to talk to you." The woman hadn't once looked directly at him.

"Why would she do that? I don't know her. I don't know anyone in Bermuda." McKella straightened her spine and narrowed her eyes. "You're making that up."

He felt the vein throb in his forehead. He pushed back a curl of hair and kept his voice low and deceptively calm. "You know I'm not."

She swayed precariously on her broken heel. "Thank you for coming to my rescue." And she turned in dismissal, limping over to the officer who'd questioned her.

"May I leave?"

He flipped open his notes, looked down and nodded. "Please do not leave the island without checking with us. We may need to ask you further questions."

"Of course."

Greg took her elbow, eliciting a muffled sound of pain. "You are hurt."

"No." She attempted to pull her arm free.

Perversely, he continued to hold her, but higher up on her arm.

"I bruised my elbow when you shoved me down."

"I'm sorry."

"Don't be. You probably saved my life."

"Let me see you to your resort."

"No, thank you." She eyed his fingers pointedly.

"Polite little thing, aren't you?"

"I am neither little, nor necessarily polite. Now let go of my arm."

Her haughtiness amused him. He liked the amber spark of battle lighting her eyes. "Or?"

She bared her teeth in a practiced expression that was not quite a smile, but was meant to intimidate. "Or I'll ask that nice officer over there to remove it *for* me."

Some of the tension left him. He cocked his head and smiled, glad to see the color returning to her face. "Fierce, too." Greg dropped his hand. "I only meant to help."

"I don't need any help, thank you."

It was a polite but firm dismissal. Too bad he couldn't *allow* her to dismiss him so easily.

"No money, remember?"

"I have money. Which reminds me..." She opened her bag and produced the bills that he had given her earlier.

He wouldn't take them. "Keep it."

"I'll do no such thing."

"You lost your wallet, remember?"

"It will be at the cottage."

"Are you sure?"

"Of course."

But her worry was obvious.

"I'd feel better if you kept the money until you find your wallet. You can pay me tomorrow."

"I may be leaving before tomorrow."

He almost smiled again. "You just got here. Besides, if one of those storms turns into a hurricane and moves in this direction, none of us will be leaving any time soon.''

''Don't say that.''

''Afraid of storms?'' Or afraid of being trapped on a small island with her brand-new husband?

''This can't be happening,'' she muttered, pushing at the strands of hair that had worked their way loose from her tight bun.

''Come on, I'll help you get a cab.''

McKella suddenly looked exhausted. She didn't argue when he hailed a taxi. She didn't even argue when he slid inside next to her. ''I'll have him drop me off at my hotel after I see you home,'' he explained quietly.

McKella simply nodded.

''You sure you're all right?''

''Peachy.''

He rubbed her forearm. Instantly, she scooted away.

''You really ought to let a doctor check you over.''

She twisted to face him. ''I don't see *you* racing to the hospital.''

''I wasn't the one on the bottom.''

It took her a moment to understand. A light pink swept her cheeks.

''I never thanked you properly,'' she said hastily.

''Nope, you didn't.'' He'd take bets her idea of proper and his idea of proper weren't on the same wavelength. Or were they? The pink color deepened.

''Thank you.'' She looked quickly away.

''Believe me, it was my pleasure.''

There it was again, that sensual tug that had no business existing in his awareness. But he *was* aware of McKella on every level—and that was stupid. Stupid and dangerous. He'd only come here because he liked her father and felt obligated to try and warn her. Now he doubted she'd listen to a word he said.

"I wish you'd let me return your money," she said.

"I'm staying at Castle Harbour. You can stop by tomorrow."

"I might not have time."

"Then mail it to me. Do you still have my business card?" He handed her another.

"I'm married," she blurted.

A tight sensation gripped his stomach, removing any vestiges of humor. She *wouldn't* be if he'd learned of the wedding in time to stop it. "I know." He pointed to her left hand and the rings that glittered there. "Would you like me to go in with you? I'd be happy to explain the situation to your husband."

"No!"

Well, he reminded himself, it would probably be tricky explaining to her new husband why she was arriving at their honeymoon retreat with another man in tow. Especially him.

"Thank you anyhow, Mr. Wyman," she added more softly.

"Greg. People who are almost run over together should be on a first-name basis, don't you think?"

The cab pulled up outside a white-brick building. A cluster of cottages sat behind it on the hillside. McKella reached into her purse without answering, but Greg's large hand closed over hers. "I'll take care of the fare. Go find your husband, McKella."

Her name came out sounding like a caress. He hadn't expected to be this attracted to Henry's daughter.

McKella fumbled for the doorhandle and scrambled from the vehicle. "Thank you. I'll repay you shortly."

She twisted away, limping to the resort office on her broken shoe.

Greg stared after her, wondering if she'd still thank him when she learned the truth.

THE CLERK WAS FILLED with sympathy—and avid curiosity—when McKella told her about the accident. She gave McKella a key and directions to the cottage. Once outside again, McKella removed her shoes and walked in her torn stockings through the lush grass to her unit. The small white cottage had a breathtaking view of the ocean.

Too bad the honeymoon was over.

Nervously, McKella opened the front door and stepped inside. The interior left an airy impression of white and soft pastels, but McKella didn't take time to look around. It was long past the hour she had promised Paul.

Her luggage sat inside the door as if it had been dropped there hastily. Only Paul's bag was missing. From the silence, she concluded he'd made good his threat to go and find her.

Gripping her bag, she mounted the stairs to the second floor. The master bedroom was toward the front and a smaller but lovely guest bedroom was on her left. She could see Paul's case sitting on the king-size bed in the master suite. McKella turned left.

She set her suitcase on the guest bed, threw her ruined shoes in the nearest wastebasket, then skimmed out of her torn pantyhose, dropping them on top. She wanted a shower and five minutes of peace before she faced her husband.

Barefoot, she padded to the door and, feeling like a fool, shut and locked it. She did not want Paul walking in while she bathed—not that the flimsy lock on the bedroom door would keep him out if he was determined.

Still trembling a bit, she stripped her torn, stained suit from her body and dropped it, too, into the wastebasket. She tossed her blouse and underwear on a chair before snatching up a sundress and her makeup kit and walking nude into the cheery bathroom.

She grimaced at her pale reflection, then tore the pins from her hair, letting the heavy mass of honey-streaked brown fall to frame her face. She fumbled with a shower cap, tucking in strands of hair with one hand as she reached past the shower curtain to turn on the tap with the other.

Her bare arm brushed against skin.

She nearly fell as she yanked her hand back. Fear clogged her throat, preventing the scream.

She expected Paul to reach out and grab her.

When he didn't, when there was no sound or sign of motion from behind the shower curtain, she leaned back against the wall, shaking with fright.

"Come on out, Paul." Her voice was unnaturally loud.

There was no sound from inside the tub.

McKella snatched up a large towel and wrapped it snugly around her body.

"This isn't funny. I'm leaving."

Silence.

The moments stretched. Surely he couldn't stand there so quietly all this time. McKella reached forward and yanked back the curtain hard enough to rip the material from the rod.

Her scream welled forth without volition.

A woman lay crumpled in the tub. She was very, very dead.

Chapter Two

McKella stared at the crumpled form and willed her
mind to function again. Slowly, she backed away, feeling horribly naked and exposed. She tucked the towel
more firmly around her chilled skin, but her eyes would
not be drawn from the deep bruises that circled the
woman's throat. The skin of the woman's face was
dark red, and her tongue protruding from between blue-
gray lips.

"Oh, God."

Her plea erupted on a sob of air. Who was this
woman? What was she doing here?

An image of the other young woman staring sight-
lessly at the Bermuda sky was superimposed. For just
a moment, McKella thought she might vomit. She
swallowed hard, swaying slightly as the room grew dim
around the edges of her vision.

She stumbled backward out of the bathroom until
the back of her knees came up against the bed. Grate-
fully, she sank down on the mattress. She put her head
between her legs until the light-headed feeling passed.

Where was Paul?

He must have gone for help. Surely the body
couldn't have been here long.

McKella decided she wasn't going to faint after all and twisted toward the nightstand. No telephone. Her heart thudded as her eyes searched the entire room.

Her gaze fastened on the closet door, and the metallic taste of fear invaded her mouth. She stared, mesmerized. The wood door was slightly ajar. Had it been that way before, or was someone staring at her through that cracked slit?

Numbing fear nearly gave way to hysteria. She stood on rocky feet. Her ears strained to catch the faintest sound. She tried to swallow and found she couldn't. Her eyes never left that cracked door. Had it opened just a bit farther?

McKella fled back to the bathroom, slamming the door shut and clicking the lock into place. She pressed her ear to the wood, striving to hear over the surging thrum of blood pulsing through her veins. If the murderer was still inside the cottage, she had no way to stop him from adding another body to the tub.

Quaking with fear, she fumbled for her sundress, needing the reassurance of clothing. She yanked the shower cap from her head, released the knot of the towel and pulled the garment on.

She turned, and her hands gripped the sink. "What am I doing?"

Acting hysterical. Giving in to panic. She never panicked. Until now. Coming in here had been stupid. If the murderer *was* inside the closet, all he had to do was wait for her to open the door.

"Oh, God."

She had never felt so terrified in all her life. Her hands shook with a force of their own. She couldn't stay here and wait to be murdered. She had to get help.

"Think!" she commanded aloud.

Her eyes focused on her makeup kit. A hair spray bottle made a lousy weapon, but it was better than a pair of cuticle scissors. Not giving herself time for second thoughts, she grabbed the bottle and flung open the door. Striding to the closet, she yanked the flimsy panel back, her finger poised over the nozzle of the bottle.

The closet was empty.

McKella dropped the hair spray. She drew in a sobbing breath and turned, flying through the bedroom door and down the stairs at a breakneck pace.

As she wrenched open the front door, she spotted the looming figure with its raised hand. Too late to stop her forward momentum, she slammed into the man full force, knocking the air from her lungs. Arms seized her, pinning her against a solid body. She twisted, wild in her panicked state.

"McKella! Take it easy!"

The deep measured tone of the command rather than the words themselves finally penetrated her fear-dredged mind.

"It's okay. I've got you."

Bewildered, she raised startled eyes. "Greg?"

He had turned them, she realized, placing his body between her and the front door. His muscles bunched with an inner tension that had him poised and ready to take whatever action was called for.

McKella stared at his chiseled features, noting a line of tiny fine scars running beneath his jaw. She slumped against him, unable to control the sudden shaking that swept her.

After a moment, he relaxed his grip. "What's wrong? What's happened?"

She shivered as one of his hands slid up and down

her arm. His touch was comforting. Soothing. Yet oddly disturbing.

"Where's your husband?"

The question of the hour.

McKella looked up, trying to summon her scrambled senses—and suddenly froze. What was *he* doing here? Two dead women—and this man at both scenes? A shiver of pure fear coursed through her.

"McKella?" He released her, arms dropping to his sides. "What is it? What's wrong?"

Friend or foe?

She took a hasty step back. Only concern reflected in those oddly colored eyes. Still she hesitated, uncertain. "What are you doing here?"

"I came to return these." Her sunglasses dangled from his fingers. "They looked like they were prescription and I thought you might need them."

For a moment, she could only stare as if she'd never seen them before.

"McKella, what's wrong? Where's your husband?" His deep voice acted as a calming balm on nerves stretched too tight.

She shook her head. "I don't know."

"What do you mean you don't know? Talk to me."

"There's a body," she blurted.

"What?"

"Upstairs. In the bathtub."

He gave her a slight shove away from the cottage. "Go for help."

"No, wait!"

But he was already through the front door, pounding up the stairs. McKella hesitated, then followed him inside. She couldn't bear to go up those stairs again, but there might be a telephone in the kitchen. She started through the living room and came to an abrupt halt.

A purse protruded from the side of the white sofa. Objects spilled from the bag lay scattered beneath the sofa. A few even rested across the room. The coffee table was shoved to one side. A lamp leaned drunkenly against the wall. The signs of disturbance were unmistakable. Why hadn't she noticed them before?

Her gaze landed on an open wallet leaning against the floor molding.

Don't touch anything.

And she wouldn't. But she was compelled forward, her feet carrying her to the wallet before her brain caught up. Then it was too late. A photo stared up at her—the implication shocking, horrifying. The room closed in around her—but she couldn't tear her eyes free, even as she swayed.

In the wedding picture, the woman in the bathtub had been alive—alive and gloriously happy. She was dressed in white organdy with a smile as dazzling as her gown. And her eyes tilted upward to stare in adoration at her beaming, groom—a man she had danced with again only yesterday.

"Paul?"

McKella forgot about the body—forgot about Greg and the reason she shouldn't touch anything. She reached down and lifted the wallet, flipping to find identification.

Betty Jane Dinsmore. In case of emergency, notify her husband, Paul Dinsmore. It was dated two years ago.

Footsteps thundered down the tiny staircase. "McKella! I told you to…" Greg's eyes traveled over her shoulder to the room behind her. Frown lines pleated the bridge of his nose. His words trailed off, punctuated by an oath as he took in the scene.

McKella shoved the wallet into the pocket of her dress. Her entire body shook.

"What did you find?"

His features were hard. Abruptly dangerous. Who *was* this man? What was he doing here?

Greg took a step forward, his hand outstretched. "You shouldn't have touched anything," he said in that quiet, calm way of his. "Let me see."

Instinctively, she wanted to retreat, but she lifted her chin and held her ground. This, at least, was something she understood. She was used to dealing with pushy men.

"We need to call the police." Her voice was stronger this time.

"Let me see, McKella."

"No."

He held out his hand and waited. The pounding of her heart left her light-headed. But it wasn't due to fear. He looked capable of violence, yet she didn't believe for a moment that he would hurt her. He wasn't going to go away. A part of her was relieved by that. Strangely enough, his presence gave her a sense of safety.

"Who are you?" she asked.

His head tipped slightly to one side. He ignored her question. "Show me what you found."

If he had threatened her, she would have tried to run. But he stood there with his hand out, his blue-green eyes coaxing her to obey. Only the pulsing vein in his forehead revealed his tension.

Her hand eased inside her skirt and pulled forth the wallet.

THE LANKY POLICEMAN'S dark eyes crinkled in concern—or suspicion. McKella couldn't tell which.

No one spoke as the sheet-draped body was carried outside. She'd repeated her story over and over again until her voice was hoarse and she was ready to collapse in sheer exhaustion.

"Mrs. Dinsmore—or do you prefer Ms. Patterson, the name you gave the constable at the accident scene this morning?"

McKella shook her head, thinking irrelevantly how alien that title was to her. She was Mrs. Dinsmore, but so was the body in the tub. A shudder passed through her.

"This woman—this other Mrs. Dinsmore—you did not know her?"

"I told you, we'd never met."

"You were married yesterday?"

"Yes, as I said."

"But you and your husband had a fight at the airport."

There was a small mole at the corner of the man's mouth. McKella focused on that. "More or less."

"About the other Mrs. Dinsmore?" he persisted.

"No! I keep telling you, I don't know anything about another Mrs. Dinsmore. I wanted Paul to explain about his references."

"Your husband gave you a reference before you were married?"

She almost laughed at how ludicrous that sounded, but it appeared she should have asked for one. "His *job* reference. When he came to work for my father's company."

"Ah."

The man put so much heart into the sound that she

twitched in reaction. Her eyes refocused on his mole as if it were a talisman.

"Our argument was personal. It had nothing to do with the dead woman. I don't know where Paul is right now, but he couldn't have gone far. The island isn't that big."

The man's head bobbed once. "True. If he is still on Bermuda we will find him."

"Well, where else could he be?"

"You have his papers? His tickets?"

McKella shook her head. "I told you, he has them."

"Including yours."

Her fingers clenched the stiff arm of the uncomfortable sofa. Freer already *knew* all this. He'd asked to see her identification in the beginning. "Yes."

"I see."

She wished she did. Her eyes flicked to Greg who sat oddly still and silent in one of the chairs across from her. His expression didn't reveal a single thought.

"Constable Freer, my husband drank too much at the reception last evening. He passed out on the bed shortly after reaching our room and his hangover was so bad this morning he could hardly string sentences together." She blinked back the memory and didn't look toward Greg. The last thing she wanted to see was his pity.

A trace of sympathy flickered in the officer's black eyes and promptly disappeared. He scratched absently at his head. "You continued this fight on the plane?"

"It wasn't a fight. I told you that. I tried to talk to Paul, but he closed his eyes and fell asleep again. He didn't wake until right before we landed. I left him at the airport and took a cab into St. George's on my own."

"Giving him your papers?"

"No. I dropped my purse in the airport. The papers must have fallen out. I'm assuming he picked them up."

"So you met Mr. Wyman and were nearly killed in that unfortunate accident outside the café."

"Yes. I mean, I didn't meet him—it wasn't an arranged meeting…he just happened to be there, too." Her heart beat a little more quickly.

"You and Mr. Wyman had never met before?"

"No. We told you that." She looked at the silent sexy stranger sitting in the corner and wondered fleetingly about the man she'd seen at her wedding. Could he be the same man?

"Yes. Yet here you both are again."

"He was returning my sunglasses!"

Unfazed, the officer studied her. "You have never seen the dead woman before?"

McKella took a deep breath, closed her eyes and shook her head. The fingernails of her right hand dug into the upholstered arm of the couch. She couldn't take much more of this.

"No." She forced her voice to sound firm and in control.

When she opened her eyes, she met Greg's steady blue gaze. It seemed to delve into her soul. Greg Wyman knew she lied.

GREG STRODE DOWN THE HALL of Castle Harbour, his fingers reaching in his pocket to produce the key card to his room. It was late—after nine o'clock. The police hadn't finished with them until almost eight. Greg had stayed until they arranged for McKella to spend the night at the same hotel where he had a room.

Dressed as a bride, she'd been a fairy princess come to life. A woman any man would want to bed. Up close, at the café, she'd been the cool professional, naturally aloof. She made him want to peel away that veneer to see if the hidden depths of her were as hot as he suspected. Then tonight, sitting on the couch facing the police interrogation, she stirred an urge to protect, yet at the same time made him want to applaud her quiet strength.

And he still wanted to take her to bed.

The lady had more facets than the diamond on her ring finger, and all of them were intriguing. Who was the real McKella Patterson, and why was he so certain she had lied to the police? Had she seen Betty Jane at the reception yesterday? It was possible. After all, it was Betty Jane's investigation that had led *him* this far.

At first, all he'd wanted was to see for himself who Paul Dinsmore really was. Then he'd mistakenly thought he could protect the innocent. Stupid. He was nobody's hero.

Greg slid the card into the slot and waited for the light to turn green. He stepped inside, fumbling for the light switch.

The blow whistled out of empty air. Something crashed against the side of his head. The force slammed him into the wall and his shoulder took a second, heavier strike. He went down, unable to prevent the fall. A hard pointed kick cracked against his hip before the attacker broke off and leaped over his body, out into the hall.

Greg fought a moment of nausea as he rose to his feet, not as quickly as he would have liked. He fumbled for the door and started down the hall after the attacker. Something warm and wet trickled down his cheek. He brushed at it, staggering into a man and woman stepping out of their room two doors down from his. The woman gasped, quickly stepping back.

"Hey! You okay?" the man asked.

Greg didn't pause. He was running—well, lurching forward—intent on catching up to the attacker. "Call security," he yelled without stopping.

A glance down showed a smear of blood on the back of his hand. He turned the corner only to see the elevator door shut as it began its descent. He was too late.

"Damn." His shoulder and hip hurt like the devil and his head continued to leak blood.

The man from the other room caught up with him. "What happened?"

"Break in," he said succinctly.

"My wife's calling security."

And security apologized profusely. This sort of incident simply did not happen on Bermuda, and particularly not at a hotel such as Castle Harbour. The police who arrived were more suspicious.

His room had been tossed. The good news was, it hadn't been done by a professional. Unless—Greg thought glumly, sitting on the end of his bed—it had been done by a professional who wanted this to *look* like an amateur job. Had Paul Dinsmore's name attracted the killers? Was this why Betty Jane was dead?

"So, you have another problem, Mr. Wyman?"

"Constable Freer," he acknowledged as the older man stepped inside his crowded bedroom. The two security men and the other policemen made room for the lanky officer.

Freer scratched at his head in a familiar gesture. "You seem to have brought some problems to our small island," he said.

"Hey, I had nothing to do with someone breaking in here."

"Really? Does it not strike you as coincidental that you are in three places in less than twenty-four hours where violence occurs? We do not have much crime on Bermuda, Mr. Wyman. It would appear that you have brought your own criminals with you."

Greg knew better than to respond to that. The officer was tired and angry. His mouth was set in a tight line that emphasized the small mole near his mouth.

Greg didn't blame him a bit. The man probably hadn't had dinner yet. The nurse finished taping the cut in Greg's scalp, then asked him to remove his shirt so she could look at his shoulder. He waved her away.

"Something might be fractured," she insisted.

He could feel the pulsing bruise. "It isn't."

"You should have X rays."

"I *should* have taken a vacation in Alaska."

"Yet, you did not," Freer stated, looking up from the notes his fellow officer had handed him. "Why did you select Bermuda at this particular time?"

He'd known this attack was going to be one coincidence too many for the police. "I'm a sucker for a crime wave and I heard you were going to have one."

Freer didn't even raise an eyebrow. "You want to tell me again that you did not know Mrs. Dinsmore before you arrived?"

His nerves tightened, but he kept all emotions from his face. He also managed to restrain an impulse to ask *which* Mrs. Dinsmore.

"Is that what you think? That McKella and I have a thing going?"

"Do you?"

"No." Imagination didn't count, which was probably a very good thing. Where McKella Patterson was concerned, his imagination was excellent.

"You do not think it was her husband who searched your room and lay in wait for you?"

That was *exactly* what he thought, and if he'd been a fraction quicker, he might have caught the bastard.

It was a nuisance to keep his voice from giving away his thoughts. "I never met McKella's husband. Why would he attack me?"

"Because you were eating lunch with his new bride the day after their wedding?"

"I was eating lunch in the same restaurant as his wife," Greg corrected mildly. "We weren't even sitting together."

"An interesting coincidence, you will agree."

Hard to argue that—since it hadn't been. "St. George is a real small town."

"Indeed. You are sticking with your story then?"

"I'm going to continue to tell you the truth to the best of my ability. Why don't you go find her husband and ask him all these questions?"

"We are trying, Mr. Wyman."

"It's a small island, Constable Freer," he said, mimicking McKella's earlier words.

"Indeed."

Hard, dark eyes stared at him as if trying to rip past his outer defenses. Greg met that gaze without flinching.

"Do not attempt to leave the island without checking with my office."

"Wouldn't think of it. It doesn't look like I'm going anywhere in a hurry anyhow. In case your minions forgot to put it in their report, the thief took my return plane ticket."

"I have that notation, Mr. Wyman."

"Great. Your man was thorough then." He nodded to the younger, impassive officer who had first responded.

"I will be in touch," Freer told him.

"I can hardly wait."

The room grew silent with the departure of the police and the hotel security men. Greg stared grimly at his rifled suitcase. Whoever had gone through his belongings had been in a hurry. Had it been the man calling himself Paul Dinsmore, or was it someone else? Someone with a much more deadly agenda?

An image of McKella Patterson rose unbidden. She was, after all, a big part of the reason he was here. Warning her had seemed like a good idea yesterday. Now he was trapped, and if he stayed, he might well be the next body for Constable Freer to investigate.

Greg uttered a heartfelt curse, rose and limped to the bathroom for a glass of water. The nurse had left two aspirin tablets, and he was going to need them.

He swallowed when a sudden thought occurred. If McKella's husband had been the one who attacked him, his next stop would be...

"McKELLA, OPEN THE DOOR."

McKella debated her options. It was obvious Greg Wyman wasn't going to give up and go away. Wearily, she rose from the chair and crossed the room.

"McKella!"

"Will you hush?" she scolded as she swung open the door. "You'll have the neighbors and security down my— What *happened* to you?" Bloody spots dotted his white shirt. A small bruise was forming on his left cheek.

"Are you okay?" he demanded.

"Perfect, but *you* look awful."

He ignored that and stared at her intently for a moment. His gaze was unnerving. *He* was unnerving.

"Are you going to invite me in?"

"I don't think that's a good—"

He pushed gently past her, his oddly colored eyes sweeping the room, taking in the details of her uneaten meal.

"Please, come right in," she said, lacing her words with sarcasm. "What did you do, rent one of the mopeds and forget to stay to the left?"

"Cute."

She watched him peruse her room, which was spacious and dominated by a king-size bed. The room also had an enormous walk-in closet and the bathroom had a bidet, but the view was far from spectacular. It did not face the water and the window was mostly obscured by a rather ugly large tree.

"Why are you here?" she demanded.

He twisted to face her and she noticed the bandage in his hair. He *had* been hurt.

"Someone broke into my room."

McKella hadn't thought she could handle any more shocks today, but this one landed with the same impact as the others. "No." The word came out a whisper.

"Unfortunately, yes. Have you heard from your husband?"

Her eyes closed to hide her dismay. She'd done nothing but agonize over Paul since the police had helped her check in here. Twice she had tried to call her uncle, but he wasn't at home or in his office. She didn't dare call her father and risk upsetting him, and

Eric Henning still wasn't answering at the number he'd left for her.

Where *was* Paul? The question—and its ramifications—haunted her.

She bit down hard on her lower lip and opened her eyes. Greg limped over to the desk, lifted a french fry and took a bite. "You're not eating," he scolded.

She eyed the cold food she'd been rearranging on the plate for the past several minutes, then returned his steady gaze.

"I'm not very hungry."

He lifted another french fry.

"But do help yourself," she added.

His grin was pure mischief. It took years from his face. Inexplicably, her lips twitched in a desire to return the smile. This man could play havoc with a woman's hormones if he set his mind to the task.

He replaced the fry and shook his head. "I would, but this stuff's cold. Come on, let's get out of here and find someplace to eat."

McKella shook her head. "I told you, I'm not hungry."

"Then you can watch *me* eat."

"I have to wait here in case Paul calls."

"How is he going to know to call you here? And when he does show up, the police are going to want to talk to him first."

She was well aware of that. The horrible possibilities had vied for dominance since she'd closed the door on her police escort. Was Paul hurt? In trouble?

Or was he a murderer?

"McKella, you aren't doing yourself or him any good sitting alone in here imagining the worst."

"What am I supposed to do?" she snapped.

"Come with me and get something to eat."

Ridiculous to feel so tempted. She glanced down at her wrinkled sundress and made a face. "I'm not dressed to go anywhere."

"You look better than I do." His stare made her intensely aware of herself and the king-size bed behind her. The room seemed to shrink until Greg Wyman was all she could see.

"There's a small bar-type place out back behind the fountain. Come on," he urged.

His voice sounded like an invitation to bed rather than an offer to go for a meal.

"They'll probably have sandwiches," he coaxed, "and I don't know about you, but I could use something cold to drink about now."

Her heart rate accelerated just looking at him. She didn't know this man, and she wasn't sure she quite trusted him, either. But she wanted to go with him—which was stupid and quite possibly dangerous.

"I'm not an impulsive sort of person," she told him.

"That's okay. I am. Come on. We need to talk."

"I must be insane."

He grinned. "Don't worry. I'm sure it's contagious. You can pass it on to someone else later. Let's go."

The bar was small, crowded and noisy. Soup and sandwiches were still available, and McKella discovered an appetite after all. She was surprised when Greg bypassed the waitress's offer of beer and chose a non-alcoholic drink, but realized that, whatever his reasons, they'd both be better off with clear heads. Greg was a quiet, restful companion once she was able to ignore her body's foolish response to having him nearby. He refused to let her talk about anything serious until after they had both eaten. Instead, they drank icy fruit drinks, ate conch stew with crunchy hot bread, and watched a group of men play darts.

When McKella set aside her bowl, she looked up to find Greg watching her intently. "Why did you marry your husband?"

His abrupt question caught her by surprise. "That's none of your business."

"It wasn't—until someone broke into my room."

"What does one have to do with the other? Paul didn't attack you. He doesn't even know I met you."

Greg stared at her. He had beautiful eyes and a ruggedly handsome, intelligent-looking face.

"The police think we're lovers," he said quietly.

"What?" Her throat constricted and she nearly overturned her glass. Her imagination leaped in a whole different direction. Lovers. The images that word invoked sent her pulse racing.

"They just haven't figured out how the other Mrs. Dinsmore works into the equation. Now, if the body in the tub had belonged to your husband, we'd both be looking at a murder rap."

McKella couldn't catch her breath. She couldn't get any of her swirling thoughts to hold still long enough to form a word, let alone a sentence.

"Did you know her?" he asked.

"Of course not!"

"But you *had* seen her before this morning. You aren't a very good liar you know."

She did know. And his quiet words cajoled her. It would be a relief to share her fears with someone. Yet she had to keep reminding herself that Greg was a stranger—a handsome, disturbing stranger who somehow seemed to be in the thick of this madness. She knew nothing about him. Besides, she was married.

"I—"

"McKella, I know you don't want to, but you have to trust me. We're in trouble here."

His lumping the two of them together like that was not helping the erratic jump of her pulse. "I don't know anything."

"Then why did you lie to the police?"

His look seared her soul, unleashing the words that had tumbled around in her mind all evening.

"I think she was at my wedding. Paul was dancing with someone right before he got sick. I didn't get a clear look at her face because I didn't have my contacts in, but...I think it was the woman in the bathtub."

Greg leaned back in his chair as the waiter set down two more glasses of juice and cleared away the remains of the meal. They both declined dessert and the waiter left them with a smile, oblivious to the tension that isolated their tiny table in the crowded room.

"Well, I can see why you wouldn't want to mention that fact to the police. It would give you more of a motive."

"Motive!" Stunned, her hand gripped the edge of the table.

"Face it, McKella. You're a murder suspect whether you want to be or not."

"That's crazy!"

"This whole mess is crazy. The police were easy on us today. They won't be so kind tomorrow after they get information from the States."

"What information?"

"You're the new Mrs. Dinsmore. The other Mrs. Dinsmore is dead. Your husband is conveniently missing. You'd better hope he turns up soon."

Fear wove its magic spell. "I didn't kill anyone, and neither did Paul," McKella stated angrily.

Greg tipped his head. "Maybe *you* didn't, but you can't be certain about *him*."

"He wouldn't. He couldn't."

"Who are you trying to convince? Me, or yourself?"

She wanted to protest, but Greg continued, leaving the sound incomplete in her throat. "We need to put our heads together and see if we can make sense of what's been happening around here." He leaned forward, his face intent. "How much do you know about your husband?"

If Eric Henning was to be believed, then she knew nothing at all. But Paul as a murderer? No. She wouldn't believe that. There had to be an explanation.

Still, Greg was right. She was a prime suspect in a murder investigation. Why hadn't she comprehended that earlier? She needed to be on the telephone—not sitting in some bar with a stranger. If she couldn't reach Uncle Larry then she'd better call Nathan Marks. Surely the company lawyer could advise her or recommend someone else who could.

Her brain had turned to mush since the wedding. She needed to start thinking again, using the skills and abilities that had made her a good VP for her father.

"McKella?"

Greg's voice brought her back to reality. She stared, seeing him in a new light. At the moment, this man was her only ally. "I hired a private investigator to check Paul's background before I married him."

"Smart thinking."

McKella shrugged. "On paper, Paul checked out. It wasn't until my investigator probed a little deeper that discrepancies showed up."

"What sort of discrepancies?"

"His last employers claim they never met the man, yet their computer records show him to be a high-level executive for their company."

"The records were tampered with?"

"If my investigator is to be believed."

Greg whistled softly and then nodded as if that made some sort of sense. "And your father owns Patterson Opticals."

"Actually, I own the company, but how did you know it was a family-owned business?"

"I did some work for your father."

The food she had just eaten suddenly became a heavy layer in the bottom of her stomach. This was one huge coincidence too many. "Really?"

Greg leaned back and smiled. "Yes, really. My firm was hired to do an outside audit four years ago."

"Your firm?"

"W.D. and L. Associates. I'm the W."

She remembered when her father had hired the auditors. That this man should turn out to be one of them…

"Why didn't you mention that before?" she demanded suspiciously.

"Because, frankly, I thought it was too coincidental for the police to swallow. I arrived at Patterson as they were wheeling you out on the gurney to the ambulance. Appendicitis, if I recall."

How could he know that unless he was telling the truth?

"Your uncle was out with a broken hip."

"Yes. He was in a boating accident the week before and there were complications with his injuries. Someone found a problem in the accounting department, so

Dad hired an outside auditor to straighten things out. I was supposed to oversee your work but my appendix picked that morning to rupture.''

"To think we almost met four years ago. How is your dad?"

Her smile faded. "He has lung cancer."

"I'm sorry. I like your dad."

"So do I. That's why I gave in to his pressure to marry the incoming CEO." She hadn't meant to say that.

His expression hardened. "Why didn't your father run a thorough background check on your husband before hiring him?"

She shifted in her chair, remembering that she had wondered the same thing when she went looking for the report. "Dad hired Paul away from Zuckerman last year—or thought he did. Paul's got great credentials."

"On paper."

She gave a jerky nod of assent. "I'm sure this is all a misunderstanding. Paul's a wonderful man. Bright, enthusiastic. Dad's spent hours getting to know him, grooming him to take over as CEO."

"Why not you? I got the impression your dad wanted you to take over one day."

She looked away, staring at the next dart player. How could she explain? At twenty-three, the world of business had been wonderfully fascinating. At thirty-two, she'd met enough challenges to prove all she needed or wanted to in that world.

"Tired of the rat race, huh?"

His perception surprised her. "Something like that. I wanted Dad to sell the company two years ago when we learned about his condition, but he wouldn't hear of it. He built it from the ground up and he wants to pass it on. A dynasty of sorts.''

''And it's your job to run it, or produce the heirs?''

''I *want* children.'' She drew back, trying to banish a sudden vision of two little boys with blue-green eyes.

His expression softened. ''What about your uncle? Doesn't he own part of the business?''

''No. He sold Dad his shares years ago. Uncle Larry is happiest working with numbers. He doesn't want to run things, either.''

''Uh-huh.''

She looked away, not liking the suspicion in his voice. The next dart player stepped forward and she took a swallow from her glass.

Greg shook his head. ''So you married your husband to please your dad.''

''And myself! Paul is a dynamic, handsome man.''

''But you don't love him.''

The chair creaked as she straightened up. ''My relationship with my husband is none of your business.''

''You're wrong, you know. While the police are eyeing the two of us as suspects, everything to do with your husband is my business.''

''That's ridiculous.''

''Really? Tell me you love him. Tell me you can convince the constable that you're madly in love with the man who abandoned you to a dead body.''

''He did no such thing. He...'' McKella took a deep breath and exhaled slowly.

''That's what I thought,'' he said.

''Okay, I'm not passionately in love with Paul, nor he with me. It's a marriage of convenience,'' she told him in exasperation.

''Not very convenient at the moment.''

She scowled, but Greg ignored her. He tapped his fingers against his glass, his expression thoughtful.

"When did you find out his credentials aren't real?"

"Never," she stated emphatically. "There's just some sort of misunderstanding right now. I got Eric's message last night, but Paul claims it's all a mistake."

"And you believe him?"

"Of course I believe him. He's my husband."

"Uh-huh."

She bristled, but he continued before she could protest.

"Why'd you wait until today at the airport to talk to him?"

"I told you, Paul got sick at the recept—"

"You told the police he got drunk."

A skittering of unease made her shift position as she thought back to Paul's strange illness. "My uncle and everyone else thought he was drunk."

"But he wasn't?"

Remembering Paul's behavior and the sudden onset of his symptoms, she shook her head. "I don't see how he could have been. Yet he had all the symptoms and he passed out on the bed."

"He could have been faking."

"No. He threw up blood."

Greg's lips thinned. A frown pinched the bridge of his nose again. "And this morning?"

"He was in a foul mood. Complained of a headache and slept on the plane the entire way."

"Sounds like a hangover to me."

"I thought maybe he was coming down with something, but—" she spread her hands and shook her head "—he seemed fine today. Just…hungover."

"Uh-huh."

"Look, I know this will sound ridiculous, but in light of all that's happened...well...I keep thinking maybe he was poisoned." She wondered what had possessed her to tell him that.

"By his other wife?"

McKella wished she had kept quiet. Greg was so easy to talk to, but there was something disloyal about discussing Paul when he wasn't here to defend himself.

"You said she was at the reception," Greg persisted.

"I *think* she was there. Remember, I didn't know about his ex-wife until this afternoon."

Greg studied her in silence. When he finally spoke, his quiet words dropped into a lull in the noise level of the tavern.

"What makes you think she was his *ex*-wife?"

Chapter Three

"Of course she's his ex-wife! You saw the picture!"

At McKella's raised voice, several heads turned in their direction. Greg slumped back in his chair, debating what to tell her. If he could confirm his suspicions about her so-called husband, it shouldn't take the police long to discover the truth. The question was, how would McKella feel toward the bearer of bad news?

"McKella—"

There was a commotion at the dartboard as one of the players scored an impossible shot to win the round. Greg dug for some money and plopped it on the table. "Let's get out of here."

They rose and wound their way through the crowd and out into the warm Bermuda evening. It was the stuff fantasies were made of—warm tropical night, gentle breezes blowing, and a beautiful woman at his side.

It was a fantasy all right, though he was pretty sure McKella was as aware of him as he was of her. He'd noticed her glances in his direction when she thought he wasn't looking. And he'd seen the subtle spark of interest in her eyes earlier. He cursed the luck that made it impossible for either one of them to act on that attraction.

Even when she accepted the truth, he'd have to curb his desire for her. A long time ago he'd come to terms with the fact that he could never have a serious relationship, never marry, never afford to have any hostages to fortune. But that didn't stop him from wanting her, or from wanting to protect her.

"I don't think you should go back to your room alone tonight," he told her, knowing she would take those words the wrong way.

McKella stopped walking. The breeze ruffled her hair, sending fluffy wisps against her face. He was glad she had let it hang loose around her shoulders tonight. The effect was softer, more womanly. The lights from the fountain reflected in her eyes, making them glitter with amber-like brilliance. She notched her chin a bit higher.

"Oh, you don't, huh?"

She could lay a man out flat with that tone. He bet she made a hell of a vice president for Patterson Opticals.

"Maybe I should call rent-a-roommate? Or did you already have someone in mind to share my lonely lodging?"

In for a penny... "Me."

Her scornful expression almost made him grin, but she wouldn't see the humor so Greg thrust his hands in his pockets and rocked back on his heels, waiting.

"Not a prayer, buster."

She turned and started walking again. He spoke softly to her back. "What are you going to do when he comes looking for you, McKella? Wait to be his next victim?"

She faltered mid-step and pivoted to face him.

"Paul didn't kill anyone."

"Maybe the police don't have enough evidence to hold him," Greg warned before she could speak, "but if he did kill his wife—"

"Why do you keep saying that? *I'm* his wife."

"Are you?"

She strode back to where he stood, anger sheeting off her in waves. "Who *are* you?"

"Now, I know I introduced myself at least once. I even gave you my card twice."

"You know what I mean. Police? FBI? CIA?"

He shook his head. "MBA, CPA."

No trace of answering humor lit her expression. "What do you know about Paul that I don't?"

Now there was a loaded question. What would she do if he told her the truth? She stood only inches away. He could reach out and pull her forward and...

And what? Prove what an idiot he was?

Greg tried to relax. Gently, he said, "He was still married to the woman in the tub when he married you."

Even the breeze seemed to still with her sharp gasp. "How do you know that?"

A group of people erupted from the bar behind them. Their happy chatter broke the hush of the peaceful night. Greg stepped forward and took her arm, feeling her stiffen in protest.

It had been a mistake to touch her. The need to do more sang through his body.

"Let's take a walk down to the pier," he suggested quietly. She held herself rigid under his fingertips. And he forced himself to remain still and not to give in to the temptation to stroke her satiny skin.

Once they rounded the bend out of sight, she pulled free. "Start talking," she demanded.

It was darker here, away from the lights. Dark enough that he couldn't read her expression—and she couldn't read his.

"I knew a Paul Dinsmore once. He was from a small town in Kentucky." She didn't comment, so he continued walking and talking softly. "A few months ago I happened to see an ad in the *Louisville Courier-Journal*. Your husband's name jumped out at me."

"What kind of ad?"

"One of the personal ads. You know the type. *JD loves KC. Please call and all is forgiven.* Usually, full names and bold type aren't used in those kind of ads, so this one stood out."

"You make a habit of reading those type of ads?"

"I make a habit of reading the newspaper from front to back," he told her, unruffled by her sarcasm.

They reached the pier where the pedal boats were locked down for the night. Nothing moved except the water, gently lapping against the pilings. McKella stepped onto the dock and came to a stop. She didn't look at the water. He knew her eyes were focused on him.

"Are you going to keep me in suspense?" she demanded.

He liked the way she met things head-on. In fact, he was coming to like a lot of things about McKella Patterson. Her mind was as incredible as her body.

"The ad said, *Paul Dinsmore, call me. There's something you need to know. Betty Jane.*"

She waited a moment. "That's it?"

"Uh-huh."

"Make your point, Greg."

"The same ad was in the *Cleveland Plain Dealer* when I went there on business a few days later."

That seemed to surprise her as much as it had him. "Did you *call* this Betty Jane?" she asked.

"Nope. No number. Besides, what would I have said? It just made me curious. Then a few weeks later, there was a new ad. *Paul Dinsmore, I have something of yours. Call Betty Jane.* I wasn't traveling that week, so just for the hell of it, I went to the library and looked up a couple of other big-city papers with large circulations. Sure enough, the ad was in them. Someone was spending an awful lot of money trying to find Paul Dinsmore."

McKella held completely still. He wished he knew what she was thinking.

"And you spent a lot of time looking into this. Why? Who is Paul to you?"

He shrugged, hoping the darkness hid how uncomfortable that question made him. "Just a guy I once knew. You have to understand something about me. I like puzzles—and this one grabbed my attention and wouldn't let go."

The classic understatement didn't speak to his sleepless nights or the gnawing in his gut that had started when he'd read that first ad. He'd *had* to know what threat lay behind Betty Jane's messages.

"That probably would have been the end of it if I hadn't stumbled across a similar message on the Internet."

"The Internet."

She could sure pack a lot of emotion into that flat tone.

"Yeah, you know, computers and—"

"I know what the Internet is."

There was no missing her haughty tone. This was a woman used to command, not a bit hesitant about putting people in their places.

Too bad she couldn't put him in the one place he wanted to be.

"Fine. I tracked Betty Jane to Lexington where she was a highly successful computer programmer." His next words were going to cause her pain, but better a little pain now, than another murder victim later on. "She was married to Paul Dinsmore. The mother of his two-month-old baby daughter."

"No."

All the air seemed to deflate from McKella's lungs. Greg reached out and grabbed for her, but she rallied immediately, pulling back, eyes glinting in the dark.

"Obviously, it was a different Paul Dinsmore."

Greg shook his head. "She showed me their wedding pictures when we met. You saw it today."

Her features tightened in obvious pain. "They aren't divorced?" she asked.

"No." She flinched, and he wished he could have lied. "I talked with Betty Jane on the basis of being an old acquaintance of Paul's. She was desperate to find him—kept telling me what a kind, considerate man he was. A wonderful husband, even if he did walk out one day—taking their joint savings."

McKella crossed her arms in front of her chest. "Did he know about his child?"

"I don't know." But he could make a guess. So could she.

"What's going to happen to the baby now?"

He wasn't a bit surprised by where her concern immediately went. "Betty Jane told me she had several sisters. I'm sure the baby will be taken care of."

McKella looked relieved. "But you didn't tell the police about any of this back at the cottage."

"No. I didn't." There were a lot of things he hadn't told the police—or McKella for that matter.

"Why not?"

"Would *you,* in my place? I don't know what's going on here, McKella—"

"So why are you here, Greg?" she interrupted. "And don't tell me you just happened to pick this island to vacation on at the same time as Paul and Betty Jane."

He shook his head, knowing how she was going to take his next words. "I won't. When Betty Jane showed up in Louisville, I followed her. She led me to your reception."

"So you *were* there!"

"Yeah, I *thought* you noticed me. I overheard some people say the two of you were honeymooning in Bermuda, so I caught a plane last night. Betty Jane must have flown over this morning."

He didn't add that Betty Jane probably wasn't the only one who had followed the honeymooners to Bermuda.

"Why?"

If she stood any more rigidly, a stiff breeze would blow her into the water. Greg released a sigh. Heck, his own motives were blurred now, but once he'd seen her husband and realized she was Henry's daughter, he'd felt compelled to try and warn her. Or at least warn off her husband.

"It's complicated, McKella."

There was a long moment of silence. McKella raised her chin.

"Why?"

This was dangerous territory. He gave a mental shake of his head. It was already too late to back away. Two women were dead because of her husband. He'd do whatever he had to in order to prevent McKella from being victim number three. Including telling her at least some of the truth.

"Betty Jane and I aren't the only ones looking for Paul Dinsmore."

McKella waited expectantly as he stared out over the moody water. Had the hurricane moved closer? Was it even now approaching this quiet island paradise?

"There's a contract on Paul Dinsmore's life," he said quietly.

McKella whispered something that the wind carried away. She turned to face the harbor, and for a moment he wondered if she was crying. He should have known better. She whipped her head around a second later to scowl at him.

"A contract. As in gangsters and hit men."

"Yes."

"I don't believe you."

Her voice was flat. Greg shrugged. "I shouldn't have told you that, but I think you may be in danger. From Paul, certainly. From those who are looking for him— maybe." Her expression remained stony, disbelief evident in the tautness of her body. "Someone attacked me in my room earlier tonight, McKella. Even the police think it was your husband. It occurred to me that you might be his next victim."

When he'd glimpsed her stepping from the cab in King's Square today, he'd been about to head up the hill toward the cottages to wait for the two of them, grateful that he'd overheard the conversation at the wedding reception about where they were staying. Seeing her alone caught him unprepared. Curiosity, and his undeniable fascination with McKella, kept him from grasping a perfect opportunity to confront her husband in private.

Instead, he'd followed McKella to the café, trying to decide whether to approach her. Once that truck had barreled out of nowhere, he'd been committed to his present course.

How could he have done anything else?

"Why would Paul hurt me?" she asked.

"Maybe he wants your father's company."

McKella shook her head. "My company," she corrected flatly. "Dad put it in my name six months ago."

"All the more compelling. If you die, who's your beneficiary?"

Contempt studded her words. "Uncle Larry. I told you it's a family business. Besides, your logic is flawed. The company is successful, but not worth killing over."

"Don't bet your life on that. People will kill for pocket change. Does your husband know the company reverts to your uncle?"

"I don't know, but what does that have to do with the body in our cottage? Why would Paul kill Betty Jane and leave her in the bathtub?"

"The spare tub," he felt obligated to point out. "Let's say Betty Jane threatened to reveal his past to you. They fight, and he kills her in the heat of anger. He didn't mean to do it, but now he's stuck with a body. He puts her in the spare bathroom until he can figure out what to do next. He doesn't expect you to find her. Why would you have any reason to use that bathroom?"

He didn't add that her husband might not have expected McKella to live long enough to see the cottage, let alone the body in the tub.

"Then where *is* Paul? Why wasn't he waiting for me?"

"Are you sure he wasn't?"

Her gaze traveled back out over the water, and he knew he'd scored a point. She didn't know for sure if anyone had been inside the cottage when she first arrived. She told the police that she hadn't looked around. Greg felt ill at the thought that he might have left her alone with a murderer.

"If he *was* in the cottage when you got there, he must have heard you go into the guest room," Greg pressed on. "He had to know you'd find the body. It makes sense that he would disappear to give himself time to come up with an alibi."

McKella shivered. Greg wished he had a jacket to offer her, or at least a shoulder for comfort. But he knew if he tried to touch her, she would pull away. She was a proud woman—bright, attractive and floundering in an environment she didn't understand.

"I'm going back to my room," she announced abruptly.

"McKella—"

"Alone."

Stubborn and loyal, and both traits could get her killed. "I'll walk you back."

"Unnecessary."

"I disagree." Steel edged his voice.

For a long minute, she measured him. Then she shrugged. "Suit yourself."

She didn't glance at him as she made her way back up the wooden stairs toward the hotel. Greg didn't say another word. She needed time to think through what he'd told her.

He only hoped she'd *have* that time.

MCKELLA ALLOWED GREG TO PRECEDE her to her room, only because she saw no way of stopping him. He checked the closet, the bathroom and even under the bed. She tried to be stoic. It wouldn't do for him to see that part of her appreciated his concern.

But his gentle touch as he turned to leave was almost her undoing. Breath caught in her throat when he stopped unexpectedly on his way out the door. He caressed her face with his palm.

"Try to sleep. Put the chain on and don't open the door to him, McKella."

She should have taken immediate umbrage. In retrospect, she did resent Greg's assumption that he could tell her what to do. Yet, his obvious concern negated the arrogance of his words.

McKella knew without looking through the peephole that Greg waited in the hall until he heard the night chain click into place.

If only the scrambled pieces of her life would click into place so easily. She had married Paul only twenty-four hours ago with the full expectation that they would build a life together—that she would bear his children. But if she believed Greg, then Paul already had a wife—and a child. And someone wanted him dead.

This was a nightmare. Paul wasn't like that. He was a good, caring man. He'd proved that time and again since her father hired him.

Would she have believed Greg if it hadn't been for the call from Eric Henning?

McKella shuddered. If any bit of this was true, Paul

had managed to hide his true personality completely from everyone these past several months. Believing Greg meant she had made a mistake of gigantic proportions, that her marriage was a horrible lie.

No!

Paul had been so kind to her father. And he'd not only treated McKella with respect, but respected her intelligence. He'd sought her advice time and again, and listened when she spoke. They had similar goals and dreams. Paul was a good man!

And wasn't that the way Betty Jane had described *her* husband?

McKella couldn't stop the soft moan that passed her lips. She hugged herself, feeling horribly alone and vulnerable. Little things—small flaws she had recently started to notice in Paul's actions, his jumpiness, his insistence she stay with her father in the days before the wedding—came to mind.

Days when Eric Henning had tried desperately to reach her.

She put in another call to the detective, but there was still no answer at the number he had given her. Uncle Larry wasn't home, either. She left another message for him, then dialed her father. She wouldn't tell him about Paul, of course. She just wanted the comfort of hearing his voice.

Helen, the nurse-housekeeper, answered immediately. "Your dad's asleep, McKella. Do you want me to wake him?"

"No, don't do that. Just tell him I called. Is everything all right?"

"Oh my, yes. He seems so peaceful now that you're happily married."

Happily married. If only the woman knew.

"I don't suppose you know where I can reach Uncle Larry?"

"Why, no. He may have taken his plane down to his place in Florida. Is something wrong?"

"No, no." Just my life falling down around my head. "I wanted to touch base with him about something."

"Now, McKella, you're on your honeymoon. You aren't supposed to be thinking business. What's wrong with that new husband of yours?"

What indeed? McKella quickly ended the conversation. She couldn't remember Nathan Marks's home telephone number, so she dialed his office and left a message for him to call her in the morning. Legal advice could surely wait that long.

When she tried to lose herself in sleep, fear was her companion in the king-size bed. McKella couldn't do more than doze fitfully, her head whirling with the things Greg had told her and the nightmare events of the past two days. Where was Paul? Who was Greg Wyman? And who could she afford to trust?

CONSTABLE FREER CAUGHT HER in the main dining room after breakfast the next morning.

"You do not look rested, Mrs. Dinsmore."

"Yesterday was hardly conducive to a good night's rest."

"Even after your evening stroll?"

She blinked back surprise, as he sat down and waved the waitress away. If he knew about her meeting with Greg, did he also know what she and Greg had discussed?

"*Particularly* after my evening stroll," she told him.

"Indeed? Do you still maintain you did not know Mr. Wyman before you arrived on Bermuda?"

"Yes."

"Even though he worked for your company four years ago?"

So at least that much of Greg's story had been true.

"We discussed that last night when we realized the connection. I was in the hospital at that time. My father hired his company. Greg and I never actually *met* until yesterday."

"So it is just coincidence that you are both here now?"

"What else could it be?" She was anxious to get away from the subject of Greg Wyman. Some cautious part of her didn't want to repeat the things he had told her last night.

The constable nodded. "What else indeed?"

"Has there been any word on Paul yet?"

"I am afraid not. How well do you know your husband, Mrs. Dinsmore?"

The same discerning question from yet another source.

"McKella, please." She met his dark shrewd eyes. "To tell you the truth, I don't feel like a Mrs. *anyone* at the moment."

But it suddenly occurred to her that this man might be able to help her resolve one issue. "Remember I told you I hired a private investigator to check into Paul's background?"

"Regarding his references, yes."

"Eric ran a routine background check, but he didn't find anything wrong." She hesitated before continuing. The officer watched her patiently, silently encouraging. "Eric left a strange message on my answering machine

Friday afternoon. He said he had some new information.''

''About your husband?'' Freer seemed to come to attention without actually moving a muscle.

''There is some question about who Paul worked for before he joined Patterson Opticals. I've been trying to reach Eric since the wedding, but he isn't answering at the number he gave me. I've left several messages with his answering service, but he hasn't called me back.''

The policeman's face remained inscrutable. ''Why do you think that is?''

She managed to control her tongue, if not her imagination. ''I don't know, but I'm worried.''

''I see.'' He studied her, letting the silence build. ''Do you think your husband murdered the first Mrs. Dinsmore?'' he asked quietly.

Her stomach muscles twisted. ''No—'' she lifted her face to his ''—but I don't know what to think right now,'' she added honestly.

Quiet descended again, the sights and sounds of other breakfasters going unnoticed.

''I will look into your Mr. Henning if you will give me his full name and telephone number.''

McKella nodded and recited the number she now knew by heart. Freer made careful notes in a small black pad.

''Good morning, McKella, Constable.''

Greg Wyman suddenly stood beside their table. His usually vivid eyes were cloudy, attesting to a similar lack of sleep. The bruise on his cheek was pronounced, giving his rugged face a slightly battered aspect. But that did nothing to detract from his good looks, McKella thought. If anything, it only added to his roguish charm.

His thick wavy hair was damp from his shower, and there was a tiny scratch on his strong jaw where his razor had nicked him. Dressed in a light-blue polo shirt and white cotton pants, he could have posed for a magazine cover—if the photographer air-brushed the lines of fatigue from his features.

"Mr. Wyman. Join us," the policeman invited.

McKella forced herself to lean back silently, as Greg took the chair next to her. He managed to sit close enough that she could smell his wickedly appealing aftershave.

"Don't you ever sleep?" Greg asked the man.

"Not when there is a murder and a disappearance to solve."

"How can we help?"

She wanted to protest him coupling the two of them together, but Constable Freer responded before she could object.

"Mrs. Dinsmore—McKella," he corrected with a diffident inclination of his head in her direction, "was just telling me that you two did not meet four years ago when you worked for her father."

If Greg was surprised, he didn't show it by so much as a flicker of an eyelash.

"That's right. It was quite a coincidence meeting on Bermuda like this."

"Indeed. The two of you had a long chat last night after dinner."

Greg flashed her an easy smile that surprised her. He projected an aura of confidence, looking utterly relaxed.

"I wish I'd known *you* had someone watching out for her. After you left I got to thinking about the attack on me. I was worried that if her husband killed the woman in their bungalow and attacked me in my room, McKella might be in danger."

McKella uttered a small sound of protest, but neither man looked in her direction.

"You wanted to protect her from her husband?"

Greg nodded. "If necessary. I like her. I don't like what's happening around her."

McKella resented being treated like a helpless female. "I can take care of myself," she announced.

"Maybe. Most of the time, anyhow," he agreed. His eyes assessed her, heating her skin. "You don't look like you got any more sleep last night than I did."

"If that's your subtle way of telling me I look terrible, then thanks."

His eyes crinkled in a smile—a slow, sexy kind of a smile that altered her breathing. "You couldn't look terrible if you tried."

Warmth swept her cheeks. She was suddenly conscious of the policeman watching this exchange. Before she could think of anything to say, Greg turned toward the man.

"Don't you agree, Constable?"

Freer didn't respond. A waitress bustled over to ask Greg if he wanted to order, and the moment slipped away.

For the better part of half an hour, the police officer continued with discreet questions—questions that might have made McKella more uneasy if she hadn't been so aware of the man at her side.

"I guess that will be all for now. Mrs.—McKella, you are free to return to the cottage. We are done with it for now."

She didn't try to stop a grimace of distaste. Greg, however, was more vocal.

"Do you think that's a good idea? Are you sending men to watch her?"

"Now, Mr. Wyman, our police force is rather limited—"

"I can speak for myself, Greg." She turned to the policeman. "I'd like to leave the island today, as soon as the credit card company issues me a replacement card."

"I am afraid that will not be possible," he told her. "We need you to remain on Bermuda until your husband is located. I am certain you see the need."

"No, frankly, I don't. My father is gravely ill. He's going to be very distressed by this news, and I've told you everything I can."

"I am sorry, but I must insist."

"What about the storms?" Greg asked. "I understand the closest one has been upgraded to hurricane status and is stalled right off the coast. I don't fancy being stranded here much longer myself."

"I am afraid murder must take precedence over the weather, Mr. Wyman. Bermuda has withstood many storms over the years. You need not concern yourself. You will be safe enough should it turn towards us."

"Uh-huh."

The man allowed a small smile that revealed large white teeth. "Tourism is our livelihood. We will not endanger anyone. It would be bad press, as you say."

"Like murder?" Greg provoked.

"Exactly." His dark eyes showed no trace of humor. "I suggest you both relax and take in some of the sights until such time as we locate Mr. Dinsmore."

McKella rounded on Greg as soon as they were alone.

"Why didn't you tell him what you told me last night?"

"Why didn't *you?*"

"They weren't my fairy tales."

"Mine, either."

He met her glare with equanimity. McKella reached for the check, added a tip, and signed her name with her room number. She was tired and furious and—if she wanted to be honest—a bit scared.

Greg covered her hand when she pressed her palm against the table, preparing to rise. His touch sent currents jolting through her body.

"Do you play golf?"

Startled, she met his gaze. The unbelievable color of his eyes was due to colored contacts, she realized for the first time. "No."

"Neither do I, but that's one of the major tourist draws here besides the beaches."

"There's always tennis and shopping if you're bored."

"I was thinking of you."

"I'm not the least bit bored." She wished he would remove his hand from hers, yet she was somehow reluctant to pull it free.

"McKella, can we declare a truce? I'm not anxious to spend the day alone and I don't imagine you are either."

She couldn't argue that. The very idea filled her with dread. She hadn't been able to shut off the chaotic thoughts last night; how was she going to cope today?

"Why don't you change into a swimsuit and we'll spend the day at one of the beaches?"

"Are you nuts? I can't just go off to the beach as though nothing was wrong."

He tipped his head to the side. "You can worry there as easily as you can here. Would you rather sit in your room all day?"

No. "That's not the point."

"It's exactly the point. We can talk and maybe piece together what's going on here."

They would have plenty of privacy at the beach for thoughts and questions, but somehow it felt disloyal going off with Greg when Paul was missing.

"McKella, unless you have some idea where your husband is hiding, you can sit in your room, lie on the beach, or we can roam the island, hoping to spot him. But the entire police force is already looking for him."

"I know. You're right. The beach isn't really such a bad idea, but I forgot to pack a suit," she lied. She couldn't possibly wear the daring two-piece suit in front of Greg. She had bought it to please Paul.

He raised a skeptical eyebrow as they stood. "There's a gift shop. You can pick up something there. I need some sun block myself."

McKella took a deep breath. She was strongly attracted to Greg. An attraction she didn't want and couldn't afford.

Going anywhere with him was probably a mistake.

IF MCKELLA HAD WANTED TO RAISE his blood pressure, she couldn't have found a better way to do it. Dressed in a one-piece bathing suit with a demure neckline, and lying under a rented beach umbrella, she was turning heads without even knowing it.

Greg shifted positions in the warm sand once more. He was sure she had selected the gold-colored suit from the rack because she thought it was the most conservative one in the store. She couldn't know that in the sun the material seemed to disappear into her honey-gold skin, leaving her all but nude against the white beach towel.

Greg had had a few bad moments watching her stroke sun block onto her arms and those beautiful silky legs. She didn't make a production of it, nor did she seem to be aware of the way the action affected him.

Apparently lost in thought, McKella didn't seem inclined to talk. She made a short pretense of trying to read, but it wasn't long before she laid the book on her stomach. Despite the sunglasses shading her eyes, he knew when she fell asleep.

Greg stretched out beside her, completely aware that he was playing a fool's game. He should be miles away. His own safety might depend on it. Anyone in the vicinity of Paul Dinsmore was in serious jeopardy. There was every reason to believe that others had seen the ads Betty Jane had placed—others who would collect a tidy sum on the death of Paul Dinsmore. They might even be on the island this very moment.

Greg shifted, wiping at the sweat that beaded beneath his sunglasses. Had Betty Jane been killed *by* her husband or *because* of him?

The hot sun and the warmth of the sand gradually leeched away his inner tension. He spent much of the afternoon watching the heavy waves slap over the flattened black slate rocks.

A sudden cry for help drew his attention to the water. Greg watched the lifeguard run into the surf. The breakers were strong, whipping in close and fast as they gobbled away the sandy beach.

Another swimmer started toward the victim. In moments, he, too, was in peril from the deadly undertow. A second lifeguard made a run for the water. That's when Greg realized the first lifeguard was in trouble as well. He scrambled to his feet and started for the water's edge along with several other men and women.

Someone began herding people together to create a human chain. Greg quickly found himself waist-deep in the foaming water, in wristlocks with two strangers. Swells slapped his chest and shoulders with each surge of the tide, but he planted his feet in the sand and held on. Eventually, everyone was pulled to safety. The lifeguards promptly closed the secluded beach.

The sun peeked from behind a growing haze in the late afternoon sky. For the first time, Greg noticed the bank of thick clouds on the horizon. He'd been vaguely aware that the breeze had picked up, but now he paid more attention. Was the hurricane starting toward the island?

Greg trudged back toward their spot and promptly halted. McKella was gone.

Chapter Four

McKella roused groggily when Greg surged to his feet. It took her sleep-drugged mind a few minutes to comprehend that he'd left her without a word. Slowly, she sat up and peered around. The excited crowd on the beach drew her eyes to the dramatic rescue efforts. The waves were wild in their turbulence. The horizon had taken on a hazy, threatening appearance, while the skies overhead remained impossibly blue with high, white fluffy clouds.

"McKella."

She twisted at the sound of her name. The gasp escaped without warning. Paul stood slightly behind her umbrella, towering over her. She was startled by the change in his appearance. A day's growth of beard accented his dark rumpled clothing.

"Paul! What—?"

"Quiet," he hissed.

She jumped to her feet, feeling suddenly nude as his light blue eyes traced her body.

"Nice. Did you buy this to wear for me—or for *him*?"

McKella refused to quail beneath that stare. His shirt was open at the neck, revealing sparse chest hairs and what appeared to be scratches on his torso. "Paul, where—"

"Shh." He looked wildly about, but no one paid any attention to the two of them. All eyes were focused on the ocean and the drama taking place there.

McKella pushed aside a sudden spate of fear. Paul looked dangerous, yet this was the man she had married.

"Hurry!" His face swung toward the beach. She knew he watched for Greg.

"No."

His head snapped back around at her firm response. "What?"

"The police want to talk to you."

Paul grabbed her wrist and yanked, dragging her toward the path leading up to the road. Shock made her stumble.

"What are you doing?" she gasped. "You're hurting me."

"Shut up."

In that moment, she wondered if he was insane.

"Let me go."

He halted abruptly, several feet up the path that led to the parking area. The beach was no longer in sight. His eyes were iced in anger, but there was calculation, rather than madness, in his expression.

"Who's this Greg Wyman? Where did he come from?"

His savage tone deepened her sense of unreality. Gone was her considerate husband—the man who spent hours laughing and talking business and sports with her father—the man who charmed everyone he came in contact with. In his place stood a stranger, a frightening caricature of the man she had married.

"Answer me," he snarled.

McKella squared her shoulders and faced him despite her fear. "Let go of me," she ordered.

For a second, he appeared startled. She ignored the wild beating of her heart to glare at him. Slowly, his hand released her. Immediately, she stepped back.

"I'm sorry," he said, rubbing at his face in a tired gesture.

McKella breathed deeply, trying to set aside emotion and draw on her professional objectivity. This was Paul. The man she had married. Was he a liar, a murderer, or the friendly but aggressive CEO she'd married?

"I didn't mean to hurt you." His hands dropped to chest level, palms out in supplication. "I think I'm losing my mind."

The gesture was so patently phoney, she inhaled sharply. McKella rubbed her wrist where his fingers had left imprints on her skin. On their wedding night his fingers had left small bruises on her forearms. And she recalled the bruises left on the throat of the lady in the tub.

The emerging pattern frightened her.

"Where have you been?" she asked, suppressing the strain in her voice.

Calculation frosted his stare. It disappeared in a flash as he transformed once more into the image he normally presented to the world. He dropped his arms to his sides, weary defeat in every line of his posture.

"Someone is trying to kill me."

"That isn't an answer, Paul."

The lines around his mouth tightened. "I've been hiding," he told her angrily.

"Why?"

"Ask your new friend," he nodded in the direction of the beach.

McKella flushed, realizing that Paul must have been watching her and Greg.

"What does Greg have to do with anything?"

"Someone had been digging into my past and following me right before our wedding. Then Betty Jane told me this Wyman guy came to her, asking more questions about me. She pointed him out at our reception. Now he's here in Bermuda with you, and I'm being framed for murder. Someone was prowling around the cottage while I was there. I barely got away before he broke in."

A hollow coldness invaded her body.

There's a contract on Paul Dinsmore's life.

Had Greg been telling the truth?

"You have to tell the police!" she told Paul. "It must have been Betty Jane's murderer."

"I think Wyman killed her."

The coldness spread. She lowered her gaze to the spot where Paul's shirt had come unbuttoned. Scratches surrounded an ugly black-and-green bruise. The marks weren't fresh enough to have been made by the woman in the bathtub.

"What happened to you?" she asked.

He hurried to rebutton the shirt. "Never mind, it isn't important. Listen McKella, Betty Jane showed up at the reception claiming our divorce was never final. I was shocked. She wanted money. Lots of it." He made a noise of exasperation. "I already left her the house and everything else of value, but she wanted more."

"You never told me you'd been married before," she accused. Greg claimed Betty Jane was searching for Paul because *Paul* had taken everything. Which was the truth?

Paul looked past her, over her shoulder, strain evident in the way he held himself, as though poised for flight. "She was part of my history—a part I was trying to forget. She had nothing to do with us."

"You only married her two years ago!"

His eyes snapped back to her face. "How did you know that?"

The flatness of his tone made her shiver. "I saw your wedding picture and the date in her wallet. You have a child."

He looked startled, then he shook his head. His tender and pitying expression was one she was becoming all too familiar with.

"Betty Jane doesn't have a child, McKella. She wouldn't have taken a chance on ruining her perfect figure to get pregnant. It was one of the reasons we divorced in the first place. I told you how much I wanted kids."

Yes. He'd said he wanted a dozen at least. They had laughed at the idea. But he had never taken her to bed. Had he simply told her what she wanted to hear?

His kisses had never stirred her to passion, but she hadn't minded. Her two sexual experiences hadn't left her craving that sort of intimacy. She was content with his company and grateful for his business expertise. She'd looked at their marriage as a merger. Paul wanted to be CEO. Her father wanted a son to run his company. She wanted children and a chance to be something other than a corporate vice president.

"McKella, you have to believe me. I don't know what's going on, but someone is setting me up."

She felt a curl of uncertainty. Paul was nothing if not persuasive when he wanted to be.

"What about Zuckerman's?"

"I told you that was a lie. Your detective is part of the conspiracy. I'm pretty sure I was drugged at our reception."

Her stomach clenched. "What conspiracy?"

But he ignored her question. "You know I only had a couple of beers and the wine we toasted with."

"You drank my glass, too," she reminded him.

"Because you said your stomach was upset. Look, stuff's been happening lately. Someone is out to get me, McKella. You have to believe me."

His handsome features pleaded for understanding. If he was lying, he was doing a credible job.

"I told Betty Jane where we were staying, but I didn't know she followed us to the island," Paul continued. "I was only inside the cottage long enough to change clothes. Then I heard the prowler and left to find you."

Confused, she shook her head. "Why didn't you report the prowler first?"

"Because I was worried you might come back and walk in on him before I could locate the authorities." Annoyance lent sharp edges to his voice. "We need to see beyond the events to find the motive," he told her. "What can anyone gain by framing me for murder?"

An excellent question.

"That Wyman guy…he reminds me of someone." Paul frowned, lines pleating his forehead. "He must have killed Betty Jane."

"But—"

Paul didn't let her interrupt. He rubbed at the bristles on his jaw, and McKella realized it was the first time she had ever seen him anything but clean-shaven. His scruffy appearance reminded her of Greg's more rugged good looks. She shook her head against the unwanted comparison.

"I have to get off this damn island."

"You took my plane tickets and my wallet," she said.

Wearily, Paul shook his head, his voice defeated. "I picked them up. You dropped them when you tripped over your suitcase. I would have given them back, but you were hell-bent on getting away from me. Not that I can blame you after the way I behaved. I'm truly sorry, McKella."

He sounded so sincere—so much the man she had come to know and like. *Could* someone be trying to frame him for murder? Greg had been at the reception, but she didn't believe for a moment that he had murdered anyone. Why didn't she feel that same certainty about Paul?

"Paul, you need to go to the police. Explain—"

"I can't!"

"Why not?"

A clutch of people started in their direction, chatting excitedly. Paul dropped her arm. "Meet me. Tonight. Eleven-thirty at the cottage, so we can talk without being interrupted." He pitched his voice lower, reminding her uncomfortably of Greg. "Please, McKella. If our vows meant anything at all to you, help me prove my innocence."

With a hunted expression, he pivoted and took the stairs two at a time, heading for the parking area above them.

McKella hesitated, and by then the crowd had reached her.

What *should* she believe? She couldn't bring herself to trust Paul completely. But she didn't know Greg.

Could they both be telling the truth as they saw things?

Paul had raised one interesting question. Who *was* Greg Wyman?

McKella shut her eyes and shivered. If he'd known Greg's name, Paul could have learned where Greg was staying. There weren't many places at this end of the island. Had Paul broken into Greg's room?

Another surge of people headed toward her. They must have closed the beach. She'd never catch Paul now. She wasn't even wearing shoes. Tonight she would confront him and demand answers. Now, she needed to get back to Greg. He'd be frantic wondering what had happened to her. Besides, she had questions she wanted answers to before she talked to Paul again.

She had to fight her way back down the crowded path to reach the beach. Greg spotted her almost at once. He strode forward, his concern plain.

"Where have you been? Are you okay?"

"Fine. I'm fine." Her body betrayed her by trembling.

Greg reached for her, and she let his strong arms enfold her. His hold was gentle, not bruising the way Paul's had been.

Who should she believe?

"Tell me what happened."

Loyalty warred within her. Paul was her husband. Greg was a stranger. A stranger who was embracing her.

"Where'd you get these marks on your wrist?"

She looked down and saw the faint bruising where

Paul had grabbed her. "Paul was here," she admitted reluctantly.

"Where?" His eyes swept the area behind her even as he pulled her against his chest, as if to shelter her. Why did his touch feel so comforting? Why did his touch spark an anticipation in her that she never felt with Paul?

"Paul says he didn't kill Betty Jane."

Greg's angry gaze returned to study her face. "Of course he'd tell you that."

"He thinks you killed her."

Greg released her. He stared as if trying to read her soul. "You know I didn't. I was with you at the café."

Instinct warned her to tread carefully. "Paul says you look familiar. Do you two know each other?"

His features hardened. "Yes," he said tersely, then turned and began walking across the sand toward their belongings.

Stunned, McKella watched as the beach rapidly emptied of people. A gust of wind swept across the sand, but her shiver wasn't caused by the cold or the stinging particles of grit. She felt nude and vulnerable in the sheer nylon bathing suit she wore. Suddenly, she wanted to be fully dressed. She followed slowly in Greg's wake.

Without a word, he pulled shorts over his navy swimsuit and donned his shirt. A number of faint scars, silver-white with age, marred his chest and back and one leg.

Questions jammed her throat, but asking Greg about the scars seemed somehow too personal. And they reminded her of the vivid scratches on Paul's chest. Were the scratches the reason Paul wouldn't let her remove his clothing on their wedding night?

She wanted to shout in frustration. Instead, she watched Greg's well-muscled body move across the sand to return the umbrella, grace and sureness to his stride despite his slightly uneven gait. He walked as if he knew exactly who he was and where he wanted to go. As if he had nothing to prove to anyone. In contrast, Paul walked with an arrogance that said, "Look at me, I'm somebody."

Why was she comparing the two men?

Because she could only afford to believe one of them.

Or neither.

They rode the crowded bus back to the hotel in silence. Greg surprised her by walking her to her room. Fine particles of sand clung to the oil on her body, making her feel gritty and bedraggled. She wanted to rid herself of the scent of the suntan lotion.

"We need to talk," Greg said quietly when they reached her door.

"Yes."

"Do you want to change first?" he asked.

She nodded.

"Why don't I meet you back here in an hour?"

"Are you sure *you* won't just disappear?" she asked.

The vein in his forehead pulsed, but his quiet voice didn't display any anger. "I'm not your husband, McKella."

"I didn't mean—"

His finger stopped the flow of her words by touching the tip of her nose. "I won't lie to you, 'Kella. I may not answer *all* your questions, but I promise, I won't lie."

She wanted to believe him.

He shut the door gently as he left.

Shaky, she gathered up fresh clothing. Then she noticed the message light flashing on her telephone. She reached for the instrument and Uncle Larry's welcome voice quickly filled her ear.

"Hey there. Got your message to call. Hope you're both having a wonderful time." Hardly the words she'd have chosen. "Your dad's doing great, but he's a little worried about that hurricane near the island. Did you know there's a second depression to the west as well?"

McKella shot a glance toward her window where the tree scraped against the glass, obliterating the sky.

Her uncle continued, "You guys be careful, now. Your dad said to remind you to use sunscreen, McKella."

She looked down at her slightly pink legs. "I did."

His voice droned on. "Paul, I can't seem to find the papers on the Tenley contract and I wanted to run some numbers. I guess it can wait until you come back, but if you have a few minutes, give me a call at the office. Take care now. And have fun."

Paul would have a fit that her uncle was tampering with the Tenley contract. Then she remembered that Paul wouldn't get the message. Not unless she met him at eleven-thirty tonight at the cottage.

There was a second message. A return call from Nathan Marks. Typical of the attorney, he kept his greeting and his message brief, letting her know he had returned her call and would be in the office until four.

McKella disconnected and dialed his number. The line was busy, so she tried her uncle's private line. That call bounced out to his secretary.

"Glory, this is McKella. Is my uncle around?"

Static filled the line. The steady thread of another conversation was clearly audible. McKella only heard part of Glory's answer. "…you and Paul were in Bermuda."

"I am," she replied. "I'm returning Uncle Larry's call."

Whatever Glory replied faded into static.

"I've got a bad connection here, Glory. Tell him I'll call back later." Frustrated, McKella hung up, hoping Glory had heard her.

She drummed her fingers against the night table. She needed information. Reassurance. Why hadn't Eric Henning called her back?

Obviously, she wasn't going to get any immediate answers from the people at home, and since Paul was being mysterious and evasive, that left Greg. One way or another, she was going to get some answers.

CONSTABLE FREER WAS OUT of his office, Greg learned when he called the police station. He left a message that McKella had seen her husband on the beach, and asked that Freer call when he got the chance.

Then Greg took a quick shower to rinse away the salt, sand and suntan lotion.

His mind spun in agitation as he pulled new clothing from the closet, trying to decide what to tell McKella. His hasty decision to arrive in Bermuda ahead of them was turning into an expensive foray. Luckily, he could afford it.

A sharp rap on the door caught him pulling on his trousers. Expecting the police, he flung open the door without checking. McKella stood on the other side, dressed in a feminine print skirt and a seductive light-pink blouse. The soft color of the material deepened the rosy hue of her flushed features. Her shoulder-length hair had been tamed to frame her face. She reminded him of spun sugar—until he noticed her grimly determined expression.

Chagrin replaced that expression when she took in his state of undress. "Oh, I'm sorry. I'll come back."

He grabbed for her elbow before she could retreat, but not before he saw the way her eyes slid down his bare chest. "Come on in, I'm almost ready. Let me grab a shirt."

She'd seen more than his chest at the beach. No doubt it was the bedroom that changed her awareness. It sure changed his. The king-size bed sent his mind in a visual direction it had no business pursuing. He suppressed a colorful image of her in that bed, freshly tumbled from his lovemaking.

"Sit down," he invited. He turned to the closet and reached for a white dress shirt. "I'll just be a minute. Freer wasn't in—so I left a message."

"You already called the police?"

"Of course."

He shoved aside a jolt of disappointment at her lack of trust, and consoled himself with the thought that she apparently didn't trust her husband any more than she trusted him.

"I wish you hadn't done that," she told him. "Paul didn't kill anyone."

Greg knew her husband's skills better than most people, but he'd hoped she wouldn't be as susceptible as everyone else to the man's charm.

"He ran away from a crime scene, McKella. The police have to talk to him."

She nodded, looking everywhere but at his chest. Greg paused, perversely glad to see she wasn't immune to him as a man. He continued to hold the shirt instead of putting it on.

"Paul says someone was already in the cottage when he got there." McKella paused for a deep breath and looked him right in the eye. "Why were you at my wedding?"

Spots of color highlighted her cheeks. Her gaze darted away from his abdomen where it had been tracing a path down past his navel.

Her unexpected question surprised him. What had Paul told her?

"I wanted a look at your Paul Dinsmore," he told her truthfully.

"*My* Paul Dinsmore? Is there more than one?"

He drew in a breath that was half exasperation and half adrenaline. "McKella—"

"Talk to me, Greg."

"I can't."

"Can't?"

"Would you prefer 'won't'?"

She glowered. "Did you talk to Paul at the reception?"

"No. I might have talked to you or your father, but I didn't see him and you were always surrounded by people. I wasn't dressed appropriately, so I decided to wait and approach your husband here in Bermuda."

"He has a name, you know."

"Yeah." He knew all right. Far better than she could imagine.

"What do you want with Paul?"

"None of your business."

That startled her, but she refused to be intimidated. "I think it is. You seem to know an awful lot about him. You even implied he wanted me dead to get my company. I'd say that *makes* it my business. Who are you really?"

"We've had this discussion before, McKella."

"But this time I want a straight answer."

"I promised I wouldn't lie to you. Remember?" She blinked at his soft rebuke. "I'm Greg Wyman, one of the owners of the firm your father hired a few years ago. I have no hidden agenda with you."

"But you do with Paul."

"Yes."

She gripped the edge of the dresser in frustration. "Why won't you talk to me? I need answers, Greg."

"Then ask different questions."

She released the dresser and took two steps in his direction. "Paul says Betty Jane doesn't have any children."

Her tone indicated how important this question was to her. She had told him she wanted children. Was that why she had married the bastard?

"I only met Betty Jane once," he said softly, and nearly gave in to an impulse to stroke her cheek. "I never saw the child, but Betty Jane went to a lot of expense and effort to locate the man she says is the father."

McKella blinked and turned away, but not before he glimpsed the anguish in her eyes. "This doesn't make any sense."

She had him there. His own actions had been stupid, though they'd seemed logical at the time. "I agree." He spread his hands to keep from drawing her into an embrace. The last thing he needed was to succumb to his attraction for McKella.

She headed for his tiny balcony and the view it offered of the tumultuous sea and the rapidly encroaching bank of low gray clouds. "I don't like the looks of that sky," she said after a moment.

Greg slid into his shirt, but didn't button it, thankful for the momentary shift in topic. "I think Hurricane Lenny is on the prowl."

She raised her head when he came to stand beside her. "Do you think the island is in danger?"

His fingers itched to stroke her silken hair. "I'm sure they'll take steps to ensure the safety of the guests if there's any danger. Freer said as much."

McKella shuddered. "I hate storms."

He could smell the clean fragrance of the scented soap she had used. The urge to tell her the complete truth almost overwhelmed him. He clenched his jaw and asked instead, "Don't tell me you're afraid?"

"Okay, I won't. But I don't like loud noises, either."

She smiled slightly, starting a new rhythm in his blood. McKella was the most tempting woman he'd ever met. Would her lips taste as soft and sweet as they looked?

He leaned forward and watched her pupils dilate as her gaze locked with his. Her lips parted the merest fraction, moist and oh, so enticing. He started to lower his head.

"Don't." Her voice was the tiniest thread of sound.

"Don't what?" he whispered against her mouth.

"Don't kiss me."

His hand cupped her face. Her skin was incredibly soft. "Why not?" He felt her tremble.

"I'm married."

He gave the barest shake of his head. "Not legally."

"I don't *know* that."

He caressed her cheek with a knuckle. "You *know*." Her eyes widened as he ran his fingertips down her neck, along the inside V of her collar. She quivered, but made no effort to step away. He stopped just short of the V's point. "In here—in your heart—you know you aren't legally married to him. Don't you?"

He felt the rise and fall of her chest as she breathed more quickly. The need to kiss her almost pushed him over the edge. Only the flicker of uncertainty in her eyes held him back. He removed his hand and stepped away.

"I don't know anything," she said weakly.

With unsteady fingers, he finished buttoning his shirt, aware that she followed every movement. "Let me get my socks and shoes on and we can go."

"Greg? We should talk about this."

He sat and pulled on one shoe. "What do you want me to say? I'm sorry for wanting to kiss you?—" he shook his head "—I'm not." Her blush deepened, making her even more desirable. "I'd like to kiss you, 'Kella. In fact, I'd like to do a whole lot more than just kiss you."

She didn't look away despite the turmoil evident in her amber eyes. This was foolish. There was no percentage in a relationship between the two of them.

"Sorry. I always did have rotten timing." He reached for the other shoe. McKella watched him warily, and he changed the subject. "Shall we take a walk? I promise to be on my best behavior."

For a moment, he thought she would refuse, then her muscles relaxed. "Is your best behavior better than what you've demonstrated so far?"

His lips quirked. "Trust me."

"Not a prayer."

McKELLA WAS AWARE that Greg studied her surreptitiously. She found this strange attraction to him frightening. She had wanted his kiss. His passion had aroused an answering desire that she had no business feeling. She was married. Why was it so hard to remember that fact whenever he touched her?

As they crossed the lobby, a familiar lanky form approached them.

"Good evening."

"Constable," Greg acknowledged. "I figured you'd call or show up sooner or later."

"Indeed. Perhaps we could go to your room and chat?"

Greg looked at McKella and shrugged. They turned back the way they'd come.

In Greg's room, Freer waited for McKella to take a seat before he zeroed in on her. "Tell me what your husband had to say."

She sketched in her brief conversation with Paul, always aware of Greg's eyes on her. He looked worried when she mentioned Paul's "prowler." She was pretty sure both men realized she'd omitted a few things, but when she finished, Freer didn't leap at her with questions.

He leaned back in the other wing chair and steepled his hands. "Interesting."

"Have you learned anything new?" Greg asked from where he slouched against the dresser.

"I learned what became of the private investigator." McKella stilled. "Eric?"

"Just so. Your Mr. Henning is in hospital. He was discovered in the car park of his apartment complex, stabbed in an apparent mugging attempt."

McKella gasped in horror.

"He is in critical condition."

Her shock and outrage mingled with sadness. She

pictured the big strapping detective and wondered how any mugger had dared to approach him.

"Maybe…maybe Paul told me the truth. Maybe someone attacked Eric to keep him from changing his story. Paul thinks someone is trying to frame him."

"Did he say who?" the detective asked.

McKella slid her glance from Greg, unwilling to repeat what Paul had said about him. "I'm wondering if Eric was *forced* to leave me that message," she mused instead.

"Why?" Greg asked.

"I don't know."

"McKella," said Greg. "His attack might have been a simple mugging. It doesn't necessarily have anything to do with this situation."

"Oh, come on," she protested. "Even *you* don't believe that. Paul's right to be scared. Someone murdered Betty Jane. And I don't believe for a minute that it was Paul."

"Not even after he bruised your wrist?"

She looked down at the faint marks on her wrist, aware that Freer was frowning. "That was an accident. He's scared. Think about it, Greg. What better way to frame Paul than to kill his wife and dump her in our cottage where she's sure to be found?—"

"I thought *you* were his wife," Freer interrupted quietly.

Stunned by what she'd said, McKella floundered. "I am his wife. I meant his ex-wife." This was Greg's fault for placing that other stupid possibility in her subconscious. "Paul told me they were divorced."

"You asked him?" Greg asked in surprise.

"I didn't have to. *He* mentioned the divorce." He had also mentioned Betty Jane's claim that it wasn't final. But McKella wasn't about to offer that—and give Paul a motive for murder. "He didn't kill her," she stated.

"He told you that?" Freer asked.

"Yes."

Greg made a derisive noise. "What else could he say?"

She glared at Greg. "You didn't see him. Talk to him."

"No, I didn't."

"And I would very much like to," the officer added. "Have you any idea where he is?"

McKella shook her head. She avoided looking directly at Greg. Sometimes she got the uneasy feeling he could almost read her thoughts.

"Paul left when the people came up from the beach."

"Ah." The policeman tilted his head slightly. "Did you hear the sound of a vehicle? A moped or a taxi, by chance?"

"No, but I wasn't listening, either. I was anxious to return so Greg wouldn't worry."

"I see."

She was afraid he and Greg saw entirely too much. She focused on the patio door, beyond which lay darkness and the sound of a wind-driven rain.

"The other Mrs. Dinsmore came from a moneyed family," the policeman divulged. "Her father owns several business ventures, including the computer company where they met."

"He worked for her?" Greg asked.

"I do not have that information yet. The Lexington authorities are investigating her background, how they met, when they were married, divorced, and the like.

We should have a thorough report sometime tomorrow—if the hurricane does not cause us too many problems.''

Greg straightened. "Is it supposed to?"

"No. We will only get the lashings of its tail, I am told. The storm will pass by the island sometime around one o'clock in the morning. The system is moving eastward, away from the island, but tornados and certainly high winds can do much damage. It is well that this will happen at a time when most of the island is in bed. You should be perfectly safe indoors, but I would recommend that you stay well away from windows in the night.''

McKella shuddered at the mental image of shattering glass. "No problem.''

"You will be happy to know that so far, your own background checks have turned up nothing untoward.''

"Naturally." Secretly, McKella was relieved to hear that Greg was who he said he was.

"Your firm is highly thought of, Mr. Wyman.''

"Thank you. We try.''

"You do much business reconstruction, I understand.''

"Well, I'd hardly put it that way, but I can see why you might.''

McKella saw him glance her way.

"You specialize in businesses that are floundering, do you not? Help them recover so they can once again become profitable? Your fees are most impressive, I am told. You leave with a share of the profits.''

McKella frowned. "I thought you did audits.''

Greg shifted. "We do those, too.''

"Indeed. Your company makes quite a handsome

profit as I understand it. You are close to becoming a Fortune 500 company, are you not?"

She sensed Greg's discomfort. His impossibly-colored eyes flashed from one face to another. "Hardly."

The policeman abruptly switched to questions about McKella's arrival at the café and what the two of them had witnessed that day.

"Have you found the person responsible for that poor woman's death?" she asked.

"No. The lorry was stolen. We have identified the dead woman, however. Her name was Eleanor Beauchamp."

There was something in his tone, something that made McKella's spine stiffen with apprehension.

"She was also from Kentucky. In fact, she was traveling with the other Mrs. Dinsmore."

The words dropped like ice in a pail—hard, hollow, and bitterly cold. McKella saw that Greg was also shaken, though he was better than she was at hiding his agitation.

"Odd coincidence," Greg said. He didn't look in McKella's direction, and her hollow feeling only deepened.

The policeman nodded. "Yes."

"Then the truck was aimed at her?" McKella asked.

Freer inclined his head. "Possibly." His tone betrayed nothing of what he was thinking. From his vantage point, McKella knew, Freer watched both of them as he continued. "She was married, but her husband was not aware that Bermuda was her destination. He believed she was visiting a relative."

McKella leaned forward, suddenly tired of this cat-and-mouse game. "What's going on? Who is this woman?"

Freer scratched at his head. "You did not know her?"

"No. Does her husband know Paul?"

"No, Mr. Beauchamp claims he does not even know who Betty Jane is. Yet the two women shared a room together."

Chills danced along her spine.

"I don't understand," she told him.

"Nor do I. However, rest assured that I will."

After asking a few more questions, Freer stood and bid them a good evening. McKella started to rise, but stopped when Greg laid a restraining hand on her arm.

"I'll walk you back to your room."

"No, I...." While his touch was disquieting, it was also soothing. She had to stop thinking like that. "Why did my father hire you four years ago?"

Greg tipped his head in surprise. "To do an audit."

"Why? I know there was some sort of problem, but we'd never had an outside auditor before."

Greg leaned back against the door frame and shoved his hands into the pockets of his trousers. "Your father didn't explain why he hired me?"

"No. When my appendix ruptured that day, I developed peritonitis. I was ill for some time."

"Oh." He fell silent.

"Are you going to answer my question?" she demanded.

Greg gave a short shake of his head. "Ask your father."

"He's not here to ask now, is he? Patterson Opticals is my responsibility. I think I have the right to know."

"So you say."

His response shocked her—until she realized he was mimicking her earlier assertion that she had only his word on the fact that Paul was still married to Betty Jane.

"I *do* say."

He was amused, and that made her angry. "Are you collecting a share of our profits for the work you did four years ago?"

"Haven't you looked at your own books, McKella?"

No—blast the man—she hadn't. That was her uncle's department, and McKella was perfectly content to leave the accounting in his hands. Her skill with numbers was based on necessity. She was great with people—getting investors, and keeping them. And while she could talk a contract down to its decimal point if she had to, it wasn't her forte and she knew it.

"Uncle Larry handles the financial end of things."

Greg's expression became thoughtful. "Still?"

"What's that supposed to mean? Now you suspect Uncle Larry of something?"

"I didn't say that."

She leaned back against the wall and faced him coolly. "You don't say much of anything. But you know who Eleanor Beauchamp is, don't you?"

"I don't know an Eleanor Beauchamp." His response was quick and sure, but his expression revealed he knew something.

"Why do you think she was rooming with Betty Jane?"

"Maybe Eleanor saw the same ads that led me to Betty Jane. Maybe Eleanor had her own agenda to settle with your husband, and the two of them teamed up. We'll probably never know the answer—and I have a more pressing question. Where is your husband going to meet you?"

McKella gaped. She hadn't told Greg that Paul wanted her to meet him. Greg was guessing, and guessing right. "Why would you even ask me such a question?" she stalled.

Greg took a step closer, making her only too aware of him again. "You aren't a good liar, McKella. I know there was more to your conversation with him than you let on."

His voice flowed over her like a warm and seductive blanket.

"It's reasonable to assume he sees you as a potential ally. You came back to the beach from that meeting declaring him innocent—"

"For crying out loud, Greg," she interrupted. "What happened to 'innocent until proven guilty'?"

He came to a stop only a few inches away. "We aren't in the United States, McKella. We're in Bermuda. They do things differently over here."

"They hang the innocent?"

He ignored her sarcasm. "McKella, two women are dead. Your investigator is in a hospital, dying. The only connection between the three incidents is your husband, and he's running free, talking about a conspiracy. But he isn't coming forward to explain things to the police now, is he?"

She planted her hands on her hips. "Stop changing the subject."

His eyes sparked dangerously, but his voice turned soft. "Is that what I'm doing, McKella?"

"Yes." She forced the word past her lips.

Now only inches separated them. She watched the rise and fall of his chest, and her heart began to pound. Meeting his eyes was a mistake. Passion lurked in the blue-green depths. She dropped her gaze to focus on his lips, only that wasn't any better. Sensuality emanated from him as if it were his God-given right.

Her palms pressed against his chest. She meant to push him away. Instead, her fingers curled and bunched in his shirt.

"No." She managed to flatten her palms. To her own ears, her voice didn't sound particularly strong, but the single word stopped him.

"Running scared, McKella?"

"I don't want this." That sounded better. Stronger.

"Marriage vows again?"

She felt his breath against her skin, stirring her desire. It was an effort to think and yet not to respond. She *wanted* to respond to Greg.

"Let's just say I take them seriously whether my marriage is legal or not." The words left her lips in a breathless rush.

His eyes held hers, the hot, hungry expression gradually giving way to a gleam of respect. "Good."

Her mouth opened in surprise.

"I like knowing you're a lady who keeps her word." His fingers stroked her cheek, trailing prickles of fire as they traced the path down the side of her neck. "So do I, McKella. Remember that."

He stepped back, leaving her breathless and shaken. Her hands dropped heavily to her sides.

"I'll walk you back to your room."

She started to protest, then saw his grim expression and soundlessly acquiesced. As they walked along the connecting corridor, she was conscious of him at her side. She tried to ignore the encompassing darkness outside, but lightning flickered in the distant sky. Raindrops splattered heavily against the glass windows.

"Would you like to get some dinner, maybe take in

a floor show or something?'' Greg asked. "It's early yet.''

She moistened her lips, tempted to tell him about the coming meeting. Too tempted. Paul was her husband. She owed him her first loyalty. "No, thanks. I'm tired. I know it's crazy after the way I slept on the beach, but I'm actually looking forward to going to bed.''

His expression called her a liar.

"Will you meet me for breakfast?'' she asked quickly.

"What time?''

"How about eight? Maybe we could go over to Hamilton. It will give us something to do.''

"Fine. I'll check on the bus schedule.''

At her door, Greg preceded her into the room and looked around. He didn't linger or make a production out of it, but simply made sure there was no one else inside. It was strange, she thought, how protected that made her feel.

He paused outside her door. "Don't let him in, 'Kella. Don't trust him. Your husband was a consummate actor sixteen years ago. I suspect his abilities have improved with age.''

His words shocked her. "How do you know that?''

Greg took a deep breath and released it slowly. "I just do.''

"You can't just say something like that and—''

Before she realized his intention, Greg bent and captured her lips in the softest, gentlest, most powerful kiss she had ever tasted.

Without another word, he strode off down the hall.

Chapter Five

As the hour drew closer to ten-thirty, McKella's edginess grew. She had changed into tennis shoes, red slacks and a matching pullover, and her windbreaker sat on the chair. She watched the tree outside her window bend and twist in the merciless wind. There was a rumbly hint of thunder, though it still seemed a long way off. Rain continued to spray against the glass windowpane.

For the twentieth time McKella put down her book without reading a page. She couldn't get the man—or the kiss—out of her head, but she'd come to a decision. She was not going to go to the cottage alone.

She refused to admit—or even to contemplate—that a part of her was scared of Paul—and maybe Greg as well. Someone was lying, and it unnerved her to admit which one of them she *wanted* to believe.

McKella snatched up her jacket, locked her door and rushed down the hall, suddenly in a hurry to reach Greg's room. Her repeated knocks went unanswered. Where was he?

Disappointment filled her. She turned away, moving slowly down the corridor. As tempting as it was to go in search of him, McKella knew she wouldn't do it.

She didn't *need* Greg. Taking him along had just seemed like a good idea. She exited the building through the main hall with an odd sense of loss.

The minute she stepped outside, a gust of wind tore at her hair and ripped at her clothing. She was shocked by the brutal force of the stinging raindrops. Had the hurricane changed directions? Was it even now heading straight for the tiny island?

McKella fought her fear, and the battering wind, and started in the direction of a parked cab. The driver snapped on his lights and the vehicle rolled forward to meet her. She reached for the handle, fighting a gust of demonic fury that attempted to wrench the door from her hands. She scrambled inside and realized the back was already occupied.

"Going somewhere, McKella?"

Shock held her frozen for a heartbeat. Greg's grim expression had her reaching to open the door again. He stretched his arm out to stop her.

"Close it."

The wind took that chore from her. Giant beads of rain hurled down on the helpless car, battering against its thin metal shell.

"What are you doing here?" She wiped at the water trickling down her face.

The driver turned to face them. "Your destination?"

"Tell him, McKella."

Greg's words were a command and a dare. He was angry, she realized. Pulling free, she sat stiffly and finger-combed her sopping hair back from her face. Her first instinct was to order him out. One look at the hard thrust of his chin pointed out the absurdity of that action. Greg would leave the cab when he was good and ready.

Besides, she had planned to invite Greg along if he'd been in his room just now. She could handle his anger.

Could he handle hers?

McKella gave the driver the address and sat back, vainly wiping at her dripping face. Greg reached into his pocket and produced a white handkerchief.

"Thank you," she muttered.

"My pleasure."

She ignored his sarcasm and used the square of linen, cursing under her breath when she realized it carried his spicy scent.

"Hiding at the cottage makes a sort of sense," Greg said conversationally. He leaned back in his seat as if finding nothing at all ominous about the way the vehicle rocked and jounced along the narrow winding roads. "Where was he before?"

"Why don't you *ask* him?" she asked sweetly.

"I plan to."

The fragile car threatened to become airborne at any moment—if the sleeting rain didn't pulverize the vehicle into the roadway first. The wipers swished futilely against the glass. Despite the headlights, McKella couldn't see a foot beyond the front of the car. How the driver kept them on the road was anyone's guess.

Looking at Greg was preferable to looking at the angry darkness that encompassed them. "Why are you here?"

He gave a negligent shrug. "I took a chance. I suspected Paul arranged to meet you. In fact, I even asked you point-blank, if you'll recall."

She fought back a rush of guilt. She had nothing to feel guilty about. "What if I'd been waiting for him in my room, instead of going to meet him?"

His lips curled upward, but it wasn't a smile. "That

didn't seem likely. He knows the police are watching the hotel.''

"And me."

"Especially you."

She swung around for a look out the rear window, but all she could see was the black rain-swept night and the wild dances of the roadside shrubbery. The car shuddered and swayed as a tree twisted and bent across the road behind them. Its branches swept their passage with an angry motion. Her breath caught in her throat.

"Don't worry," Greg said, his voice so low she had to strain to hear him. "The police have better things to do tonight than to follow us. The hurricane is going to pass directly to our north in less than an hour."

"Constable Freer said not before one o'clock."

She heard the thread of nervousness in her voice. So, apparently, did Greg. His anger softened and he rested a warm hand against her cool, damp one. "Someone forgot to tell Mother Nature the timetable. Lenny is gaining strength and speed a lot faster than before. I'm worried it could change course and head right at us."

"There's a cheery thought."

He squeezed her fingers in comfort and a long branch flew across the road in front of them. The driver braked and swerved to avoid it, muttering something sharp under his breath. Greg squeezed McKella's hand again, and she flashed him a grateful smile. No matter how at odds they were, she was thankful for his presence. She settled back, trying for a calm she couldn't possibly attain.

"Why are you doing this? Why are you going with me?"

He rubbed the side of his face in a tired gesture. "I don't know. I must be crazy."

McKella had a strong urge both to smile at his words and to touch him reassuringly. She pushed aside both impulses. She was married. To a very nice man. Who might also be a bigamist and a murderer.

When they finally arrived, Greg asked the driver to wait. But the man shook his head and pointed to his watch. "Two minutes," he told them. "No more."

The storm drove them to the front door, flogging their backs. The reduction of sound and fury inside the cottage was incredibly welcome. The evil darkness was not.

"Paul?" McKella shivered, straining to hear above the storm. "Paul, it's McKella."

The cottage remained ominously silent.

Greg fumbled for a light switch. The soft glow of the table lamp made things worse by casting long shadows against the walls and ceilings.

"Paul?"

Greg began turning on lights. The more the better in her opinion.

Someone had cleaned. There were no signs that anything had ever been amiss inside the small cottage. In the kitchen, Greg opened cupboards and began removing bowls and pans.

"What are you doing?"

He filled a saucepan with water. "Getting prepared."

"Prepared for what? We aren't staying here. We're going back to Castle Harbour as soon as we talk to Paul."

Greg shook his head. "If he's not here now, he isn't coming, McKella. Listen to that wind."

As though she could do anything else. It was a malevolent, forbidding sound.

"I am not sleeping here," she stated firmly.

"Good thing you took a nap earlier then. You'd better invite the driver inside if he hasn't already left. Then see if you can find a flashlight or some candles."

McKella bit back an angry retort as the windows rattled desperately. A glance outside showed the cab had gone.

"He left. You knew this was going to happen."

"Not exactly, but it doesn't surprise me." Greg looked up from filling the sink. "Did you find any candles?"

She cringed at a loud blast of thunder.

"Check down here," he suggested kindly. "I'll go up and look around. Light a candle right away if you find any. I don't think the lights are going to last much longer."

She stopped him with a hand on his forearm. "Don't go up there." To her own ears her voice sounded high and strained.

Greg looked from her hand to her face. He reached out to stroke the line of her jaw. "One of us has to."

"Why?"

"We have to be sure he isn't up there, McKella."

She swallowed past the dryness in her throat. "Then I'll go with you."

"Your choice, but we're going to be sitting in the dark any moment now if we don't find candles soon."

Wind buffeted the walls for punctuation. McKella released him and turned away. "Hurry."

"I will."

She flung open the nearest kitchen cupboard and peered inside, listening to Greg's footfalls as he headed for the steps. She tried to convince herself everything would be all right. They were safe here.

But she opened the second drawer three times before she actually took note of what she was seeing. There were two emergency candles and a pack of matches. There was also a long-bladed knife.

GREG FLICKED ON LIGHTS as he mounted the stairs. The house groaned in protest of the wind's abuse, effectively masking any other sounds. He didn't really think the bastard was in the cottage. The bungalow felt too empty for that, but McKella's husband was a tricky son of a bitch.

The spare bedroom was clean and empty. No sign that a corpse had ever been in the bathroom. The master bedroom was just as sterile. The drapes were closed, hiding the balconies and their turbulent views. The beds were neatly made, the closets and drawers empty.

"Greg? I found two candles."

He snatched towels from the bathroom, tugged the comforter and blankets from the bed, grabbed two pillows, and headed for the stairs with a nagging sense of unease—like he'd left something undone.

"Greg?"

"Coming."

"What are you doing with those?" she asked, meeting him at the foot of the stairs.

"Did you plan to sleep upstairs?" he asked.

She shuddered. "I told you, I don't plan to sleep at all."

"Too bad. I was going to share."

Lightning split the sky, visible right through the heavy draperies. A vibrant clash of thunder immediately followed. McKella jumped. The candle quivered. The lights remained on.

"You know," Greg said conversationally, moving

to stand within touching distance of her, "the bad thing about this cottage is the view."

"What?"

Her voice wasn't quite steady, he noted. Neither was her hand, but she didn't look to be on the verge of hysteria. McKella was made of sterner stuff.

"Too many windows," he said pointedly. "We need to get away from them."

McKella peered around, her body rigid with tension. "How about the kitchen?" she suggested. "Over by the patio? The storm seems to be hitting hardest against the front door."

"Good idea." He handed her a towel and dropped the rest of the items on the floor. Then he went back for the chair and couch cushions.

"What are you doing?"

"Well, you can sit at the table if you want to, but I'd prefer to be under it." He dumped the cushions on the floor and pulled the chairs away from the table.

"You're kidding."

"Nope. This table isn't much, but it will offer some protection from flying glass."

"You know you're scaring me half to death, don't you?"

Her eyes were round with the nervousness she was tightly controlling. He started to say something teasing, then spotted the knife. He lifted the blade from the counter, tested it in his hand, and eyed her steadily. "Planning my demise?"

McKella looked sheepish. "It was in the drawer with the candles."

"Uh-huh."

He moved the table away from the window and over against the pantry. The knife, he handed to her. She immediately set it on the table while he began laying the cushions underneath.

"What are you doing?"

"Making up a bed. We could lose the lights any—"

Lightning and thunder cracked simultaneously. The house quaked and plunged into sudden darkness. McKella peered at Greg over the single flickering candle in her hand.

"I'll take one of the pillows," she informed him.

THEY RECLINED ON THE CUSHIONS, with the blankets curled about them to ward off the chill of their damp clothing. The table made a cozy cave-like shelter, Greg decided. A bit cramped, but with McKella sitting next to him, he wasn't complaining.

They had shed their sodden jackets and used the towels to blot up as much moisture as they could. Greg would have liked to remove his wet pants, but he suspected that wasn't an option. On the other hand, McKella might not even notice. Her fists were clenched so tightly her knuckles were white.

He saw her shiver and circled her damp shoulders with his arm. "Come'ere."

"Greg…"

He tucked the blanket up around her chin. "I'm just going to hold you to warm you up."

She slanted him a speculative look that made his heart beat a little faster. "I'm not cold."

"Okay, then you can warm *me* up. I need lots of heat." He grinned and tugged her a little closer so her head rested beneath his chin.

"You need a cold shower."

But he sensed her smile and she didn't pull away.

As thunder deafened the heavens, he savored the scent of her shampoo.

"You smell good," he told her.

She tensed, but then relaxed. "I hate storms."

"I can tell."

She lifted her head to look at him. "Am I acting like a baby?"

"Nope. You're keeping *me* from acting like a baby. If I didn't have you to hold, I'd curl up in a fetal ball until this was all over."

"Ha. Nothing seems to scare you." But she smiled and settled back against his chest.

Greg started to tell her his bravado was just an act, then stopped, straining to hear above the storm. Were those footsteps overhead?

A boom of thunder made them both jump. He stroked her arm gently as he strove to listen. The feeling of having left something undone nagged his conscience.

"What's wrong?" she asked.

He dropped his other hand to her blanket-covered thigh to distract her. Unfortunately, she wasn't the only one it distracted. "You mean besides a hurricane outside our door?"

She lifted his hand and moved it back onto his own leg. "Behave."

He smiled down at the top of her head. "Darn. Okay, tell me what you like to do for fun."

"A question for a question?" she asked.

"Okay."

She was silent a long moment as if collecting her thoughts. Once again, he thought he heard something overhead—a creak that didn't sound like the others. He waited, but there was no other noise beyond what he'd come to expect from the storm.

"I'm a homebody, I guess. When I'm not working I like to read or paint."

She tipped her head back to look at him, exposing the gentle curve of her throat. He had a strong desire to lay kisses along that column of flesh.

"What do you paint?" he asked quickly.

"Watercolors, mostly. My dad bought me my first paint set to keep my crayons away from the walls."

"Headstrong even then, huh?"

"I prefer to think of myself as strongly independent. What about you, what do you like to do?"

Greg tensed again. Surely those noises had been the floorboards creaking under the weight of the storm. He'd checked the upstairs thoroughly. No one else could be inside. Unless there was an attic...

"Well?" she asked.

"Well, what?"

"Greg, is something wrong?"

Of course there was no attic. These were summer cottages, not homes. He didn't want to scare her. "I'm an avid reader, too," he admitted, "but I spend a lot of my free time exploring my computer."

"Surfing the Internet?"

The messages he had seen on-line for Paul Dinsmore popped into his thoughts, making his agreement a low sound of assent.

"Not a party person then?" she pursued.

"Nope. I prefer quiet evenings with friends, concerts, plays, that sort of thing."

"Me, too," she agreed.

"Is that why you got married?"

Instantly, she tried to pull away, but he tightened his hold. "I'm curious, McKella, not trying to pry."

"Are you related to Paul?"

"Related?" The unexpected question jump-started his nerves. "Where did you get an idea like that?"

She shifted free of his embrace, letting the blanket drop to her lap. "You're built like him. Same hair, similar body type. You even move a lot alike."

He knew. He just wished *she* hadn't noticed. "McKella, if you'd like to see my birth certificate—"

"That doesn't answer the question, Greg. Why are you keeping secrets?"

McKella was too bright by half, and her questions were moving in a dangerous direction. His safety and hers depended on keeping his past well buried.

"Do you want me to lie?"

Her chin jutted forward. "No."

"Then I can't explain what I'm doing here, or why I know what I know." He sighed and shut his eyes, running a tired hand along his jaw. He should have been better prepared for this inquisition.

"I wish we had met four years ago."

"You're changing the subject again."

"Uh-huh."

"Why?"

He deliberately misinterpreted her question. "Because if I'd met you four years ago, you never would have been sitting around waiting—ripe for that bastard."

Her lips parted in surprise. He was more than a little surprised himself. That hadn't been what he'd intended to say.

"Sitting around waiting? How flattering to know that's what I've been doing all these years."

He'd put his foot in it this time. "I didn't mean—"

A powerful fist of air shook the house, followed by a colossal clap of thunder. McKella jumped. Greg's hand came to rest on the rise of her breast.

Their eyes locked. An answering excitement sparkled in her eyes, quickly buried under the downward sweep of her lashes. "Move it or lose it," she warned.

"Do you really mean that?"

"I'm still wearing a wedding ring," she reminded him, wiggling the offending appendage.

"The problem is, I don't care."

He heard her indrawn hiss of air, but his declaration was no more than the truth. He raised his hand to her shoulder. "I don't consider your marriage real, remember? You were tricked. The union is fake."

"I wasn't tricked, Greg. I took those vows with my eyes open."

"So you thought, but he was already married."

"He says they were divorced. I—"

This time the sound was unmistakable. His hand whipped out to cover her lips and still her words. Even over the continuous roar of the storm, Greg heard the distinctive creak of the top step.

They weren't alone in the cottage.

"Where'd you put the knife?" he whispered. And in that nanosecond, he remembered what he had left undone upstairs. He hadn't checked the balconies.

"What's wrong?" she breathed.

"Someone is in the house. Stay here."

She grabbed his arm to hold him in place. They both knew there was only one person who could be inside the cottage. Greg fumbled for the knife, nicking his finger on the sharp blade as he handed it to her.

"Keep this out of sight unless you need it."

McKella scrambled forward, but he motioned her back and slipped from the room. Lightning flashed, briefly illuminating the interior. A shadowy figure moved—less than three feet away. Greg lunged, and they went down in a rough tangle of arms and legs.

Greg managed to land a satisfying blow to the intruder's midsection. Air whooshed from the man as Greg followed up with a fist to the jaw.

"Cool it, *Paul*," he growled, emphasizing the name.

The sodden wet body under his went completely still. In a burst of vivid lightning, Greg saw the blue eyes widen.

"It *is* you!" he gasped. "But you're dead!"

"Disappointed?"

A fist connected with his kidney and Greg slumped to one side. His opponent scrambled to his feet. Greg rolled to the side in time to avoid some of the kick's force, but air still rushed from his lungs as a heavy shoe slammed into his back.

"Paul!" Lightning illuminated McKella, who stood a few feet away. "Stop it! Both of you, stop it!"

Her husband pivoted towards her, a tower of rage. Greg surged to his feet. McKella brought up the knife.

"Stop!" Her voice was firm—in command. She held the knife like a fighter, tight against her body, her weight forward on the balls of her feet.

"Think those self-defense classes mean you can take me, McKella?" her husband snarled.

"Yes."

From her tone and her stance, Greg wasn't sure that she couldn't—but he wasn't taking any chances. He launched himself, catching his opponent off guard. They crashed into the coffee table and careened off an overstuffed chair.

"Stop it!"

Greg ducked a fist aimed for his eye and caught his opponent on the chin. He landed his next blow as well and had the satisfaction of watching the bastard crumple to the carpet.

Greg followed him down, grabbed him by his sodden jacket and shook him with barely contained temper. "Why did you kill Betty Jane?" he demanded.

Lightning sizzled overhead. The cottage shuddered. Blood trickled down the other man's chin from his split lip. Greg read pure hate in his expression and knew his accusation of murder was correct.

"And Eleanor?" Greg demanded.

"Who?" Blue eyes stared at him in total bewilderment.

"Eleanor *Miller.*" Deliberately, Greg used her maiden name. "Outside the café."

The fallen man uttered a surprised epitaph. "I don't know what you're talking about."

His eyes said he knew exactly who Eleanor Miller Beauchamp was, but a growing roar stopped Greg's next question. Greg lifted his head. The rush of sound matched the clamor of a freight train plunging straight for them. In the back of his mind, he'd heard the sound building, felt the pressure changing. Only now did he realize the meaning. A tornado was coming right at them.

"McKella!" He released her husband and threw himself at her, tumbling them both to the couch. The world exploded in unbelievable sound and fury.

McKELLA THOUGHT THAT SHE MUST have blacked out. An immovable weight pressed on her chest, making breathing difficult. Rain pummeled her open eyes, stinging her cheeks. She blinked furiously before she realized that Greg lay across her body, totally inert. For a terrified second she thought he was dead.

"Greg?"

He stirred and moaned.

"Greg, wake up! You have to wake up!"

The storm had not lessened and now there was no roof to protect them. It took a minute for her fogged brain to comprehend that the entire upstairs of the cottage was gone. So was the side wall. The front had crumpled inward. Ignoring the blinding rain, she pushed against Greg's weight, trying to lift her head for a better view.

Greg lay pinned by one of the wing chairs. Miraculously, they were still on the couch and it was still upright. He stirred again.

"Greg?"

Blue-green eyes drifted open.

"Greg? Can you move?"

He swallowed and tried to shift positions. "Maybe tomorrow," he muttered and closed his eyes.

"Greg! Don't you dare pass out!"

"Knew you were the bossy sort."

His eyes blinked open and this time relief slid through her as they focused on her face.

"What hit me?" he muttered.

"Most of the house."

That got his attention. Weakly, he pushed himself upward, dislodging the chair from his back. She could breathe more easily without his weight bearing her into the springs of the lumpy couch, but the wind sucked away most of her oxygen.

Greg muttered a fervent oath as he surveyed the shambles of the once-cozy cottage.

Their couch rested against what had been the back wall of the kitchen. When the front of the cottage had collapsed inward, it had showered them and the ground with all manner of debris. The staircase leaned drunkenly, leading only to the demented sky. Angry lightning whipped across that sky as it sluiced torrents of water down on them. Thunder echoed in their ears.

Greg tottered forward a step. Glass crunched beneath his shoes. McKella accepted his hand and stood as well, thankful that she could. In her left hand she still held the long-bladed kitchen knife. It was a miracle she hadn't cut one of them with it.

"Paul!" she exclaimed.

Greg swung his head around and nearly fell over, then steadied himself. "Where?"

"He must be here somewhere."

Without warning, every hair on her body rose in alarm. Lightning plunged to earth yards from where they stood, so dazzling in its brilliance that she was momentarily blinded and totally deafened by the immediate thunderclap. McKella could almost taste the ozone.

She dropped the knife. "Come on!"

Greg swayed and nearly went down again. She slid her arm around his waist, stumbling as he allowed her to help support him. That, in itself, told her he was hurt.

To their left, one cottage stood intact. She didn't think they'd make it, but she had to try.

With every step, the wind buffeted them, and her mind did battle with sheer terror. Her horror of storms, her distorted memory of those seconds just before the tornado struck, and her absolute fear that another twister would drop down to finish the job, would have paralyzed her if Greg hadn't leaned so dependently against her. She had to get him to safety.

Crossing the yard took forever. Somehow, they reached the quasi-haven offered by the other patio. She pounded on the glass door, but no one answered. Greg slumped against the wall, and that fueled her fear.

Leaving him, she grabbed a brick from some rubble and she heaved it with all her strength at the sliding glass door. The glass cracked. The brick bounced away, and McKella went after it.

Greg lurched erect. He swayed toward her as she prepared for another throw.

"Let me," he yelled.

"You'll fall down."

"Probably."

He took the brick and hurled it. The brick sailed through the glass, the sound buried under the crack of thunder. Greg's knees started to buckle, but with her support he managed to stay upright.

"Watch your hand," he cautioned, as she fumbled to unlock the door.

"Quiet, hero. This is my rescue."

"Uh-huh. And a terrific job you're doing, too."

"Yeah, right."

They staggered inside the cottage, which was a mirror image of the one they'd left.

"Anybody home?"

Only the storm responded.

Greg suddenly pulled away, stumbled for the kitchen sink and vomited. McKella's own stomach churned in reaction, but she followed him, stroking his back until he finished.

Wasn't that a sign of a concussion? Oh, God.

"Sorry," he muttered.

"Don't apologize." She offered him a paper towel from the roll on the counter. "Come on. You have to make it to the couch before you pass out."

He gave her a sickly smile. "Bossy."

"Yes."

"Let me rinse my mouth first." He pulled a glass from the cupboard, swaying weakly.

"Greg…"

"I'm fine. Really."

She doubted either of them could have made it farther than the couch. Greg collapsed on the sofa and promptly shut his eyes. She slid down on the carpet next to him.

"Don't you dare have a concussion," she told him. "Okay."

But he didn't open his eyes.

The windows rattled. The cottage shuddered. Was the storm getting worse? she wondered. Was another tornado about to strike? Should she build them a barricade using the two chairs in case the windows went?

Greg laid a hand on her shoulder. "You doing okay?"

"Peachy."

The comfort of his touch soothed her growing panic. They had survived a tornado. They would survive the rest that Hurricane Lenny threw at them.

"Is that a dish of mints on the table?"

An obliging flash of lightning revealed the wrapped candy sitting in a glass bowl on the coffee table. "Want one?"

"Please."

She unwrapped a candy and handed it to him. "What about Paul?" Had he been killed? Or was he still in the rubble of the other cottage, trapped—maybe dying.

"Do you still have the knife?"

"No." She thought he cursed. Greg started to sit up and she pushed him firmly back against the couch. "You aren't going anywhere."

"He might come back." Greg gripped her shoulders.

"Then we'll deal with him."

The grip weakened. "He's dangerous."

"It will be okay."

God help her, she prayed that was the truth. The intensity of Paul's rage had astonished her. In those moments when he faced her, she had known he was dangerous in the way any cornered animal is dangerous. She had never really known her husband at all, she realized. She didn't want to *believe* that Paul had killed Betty Jane, but her belief now lacked conviction.

How long she and Greg huddled there in silence, she wasn't sure, but after awhile, it seemed that the wind wasn't quite as strong, that the cottage didn't shake as badly. She became aware of how miserably uncomfortable her sodden clothing felt. And she grew increasingly worried about Greg. He hadn't stirred for some time.

McKella removed his limp hand from her shoulder and rose to her feet. Greg blinked open bleary eyes. "Wha's wrong?" he asked groggily.

"I'm going to have a look around."

"No!" He labored to sit up.

"Greg, it's okay. I just want to see what we're dealing with here."

That appeared to bring him to his senses quickly enough. "Absolutely not!"

She rested a hand on his shoulder. "Don't worry, I'll stay well back from the windows."

"Damn it! I'll come with you." He sat up despite her attempt to restrain him.

"Don't be silly. You can hardly walk."

He swung his feet to the floor, grimaced, and gave her a determined look. "I can walk." His hand gingerly felt for the back of his head.

"How bad is your head?"

He muttered something indistinguishable.

She bent over, pushing aside his hand. An enormous welt met her probing fingers. Greg sucked in a painful breath.

McKella swallowed fear. "You need a hospital."

"Want to call a cab?" he suggested wryly.

"Funny man. Maybe I'd better have a look at the rest of you."

Despite his obvious pain, his eyes held a dull gleam that she recognized.

"Talk about wish fulfillment."

"You're in no condition for those sorts of thoughts."

"You haven't even looked yet." But pain colored his voice.

"Keep teasing, but tell me where you hurt."

"Any minute now my head's going to fall off and roll on the ground."

"Delightful image. I have some aspirin in my purse." She paused and almost snorted in disgust. "Unfortunately, I have no idea where my purse is right now."

"Probably the middle of the ocean."

"You may be right. Does anything else hurt?"

"Besides my pride?"

"Greg—"

"You want a list? I think the chair left its mark on

my back, and your so-called husband landed a terrific jab to my kidneys, not to mention nearly breaking my jaw. Other than that, I think I'll live." His eyes fastened on her. "What about you? Are you okay?"

McKella smiled. "Thanks to you, I'm fine. You did a good job in the hero department."

"So did you."

His gaze warmed her, even as his touch had done. She laid a hand along his jaw, feeling the stubble. He turned his head and kissed her palm.

"I'm glad," he told her. "I'm very glad."

The words disoriented her. Mesmerized by the intensity of his expression, she could only shake her head, suddenly conscious of her bedraggled state. Her jacket had been lost along with her purse, her hair hung in dripping tangles about her face, and her clothing was plastered against her cold, wet body. Yet he looked at her with such heat that it was unnerving.

"Greg, you're too injured to be thinking about sex."

The smile that slashed his face was wickedly compelling. "I hope I'm never *that* injured." He pulled her head down toward his lips. McKella didn't resist.

His lips brushed hers with tantalizing slowness, and she tasted the peppermint he'd eaten. His finger pressed against the corner of her lips and she parted them to allow his probing tongue entrance. The kiss was unlike any other. She was startled anew by the excitement he created. Her hands gripped his shoulders when he pulled her to stand between his legs.

"Hey! Anybody in here?"

The shout jolted her. Adrenaline pumped through her body. She swung her head in an arc, looking for a weapon as a flashlight pinned them in its beam. Behind the light stood a tall wet figure dressed in a long yellow slicker.

Her hand closed over the nearest lamp, even as Greg rose to place himself between her and the newcomer.

"You folks okay?" the voice asked.

Tension drained from Greg's posture. Her own shoulders sagged in relief. She set the lamp back on the table, as Greg shot her a quick, droll smile.

"Almost," he muttered dryly.

Chapter Six

They left the Hamilton hospital in the early hours of the morning. Wind gusts still surprised the unwary, and rain dripped in a steady rhythm—but the worst was over.

Fallen trees and other debris littered the silent streets. The cabby who took them back to Castle Harbour talked almost nonstop about the storm and its effects.

"Lots of excitement," he told them cheerfully. "The harbor is closed in St. George. The docks took a hammering. And we lost our trunk lines."

"Trunk lines?" McKella asked.

"Telephone connections overseas are down," Greg translated.

The driver beamed agreement. "Not to worry, repairs won't take long." He flashed them another wide grin. "The power station was damaged, too."

Greg sighed. "No electricity?"

"Not to worry," he repeated. "We're used to storms. Hamilton doesn't look too bad, does it?"

Their eyes were drawn to the empty storefronts carefully boarded against the storm. The deserted rain-swept streets had a surreal, ghostly feel to them in the gray, morning light.

"The north end of the island took the brunt of the storm," the cabby continued. "There was even a tornado funnel sighted."

Greg squeezed McKella's hand. She offered him a wobbly smile in return. "You should have stayed in the hospital," she muttered.

"With some unfeeling nurse—when I can have you tending my every need?"

"In your dreams." But relieved by his resiliency, she widened her smile. When he'd collapsed after the rescuers arrived, she'd been certain he would die from a concussion.

He must have read her mind again, because the deep timbre of his voice became softly intimate. "I'm fine, McKella. A slight concussion is nothing. I've had worse playing touch football."

"So you said."

His thumb stroked the skin of her hand. "The doctor agreed."

"The doctor barely spoke English."

The vehicle rolled to a sudden stop. Workers clustered in the middle of the roadway with chain saws, cutting away at a hapless tree spanning the street. "Right back," the cabby promised. He flung open the door and scurried over to join the others.

Exhausted, McKella leaned back against the seat cushion and closed her eyes. "What do you think happened to Paul?"

"Do you want my hopes, or a serious answer?"

She opened an eye to glare at him.

Greg heaved a gusty sigh. "Okay, at a guess, he got away and crawled back under some rock to hide."

Shocked, McKella tugged her hand free and sat up

straight. "Greg! Paul may be dead, or lying somewhere injured."

"No such luck."

Remembering their confrontation at the cottage, McKella studied his drawn features. "Why do you hate him so much?"

"Practice," he muttered and closed his eyes. "In case you haven't figured this out yet, your husband only pretends to be a nice person."

McKella decided not to argue. Greg didn't look as if he could go three rounds with a kitten at the moment. "You said there's a contract out on him."

"I said too much."

"Is there?"

"Yes."

His response was barely audible. She probably shouldn't tire him with questions right now. He was hurt. He was fatigued. His defenses were down.

Perfect timing.

"What did he do?"

Greg sighed and opened his eyes. "Paul Dinsmore witnessed a crime and testified about what he saw."

"Now that, I can believe. That's the side of him I've seen, Greg. The kind, considerate man who befriended my father and asked me to marry him."

He shook his head and winced. "He testified in exchange for immunity, McKella. He'd broken into a warehouse bent on larceny."

"Oh."

"He got trapped inside and watched a small-time hood kill a business associate. Unfortunately for Paul, the killer had connections and his connections took umbrage to one of their own serving a life sentence—and probably to the fact that Paul broke into their warehouse in the first place. They took out a contract as an example to others.'' He yawned and then continued. ''Those things don't have expiration dates, you know. Three months, twenty years, it's all the same. Either the contract is pulled or the hit is completed.''

Exhaustion smudged his eyes and drew the skin tight over his cheekbones. Still, McKella couldn't stem the flow of questions eating at her. ''How do you know all this?''

''I made it my business to find out.''

''Why?''

''For reasons of my own. McKella, your kind, considerate, bigamist of a husband married you, fully expecting to inherit the reins of a profitable company on the verge of a major breakthrough,'' he explained patiently.

Surprised, she leaned toward him. ''You know about that?''

''I'm a businessman. I read the papers. Patterson Opticals is on the cutting edge. Ben Kestler is a clever young researcher bordering on genius. Your father made a real coup getting him on your team.''

''I hired him.''

Greg raised an eyebrow. ''Your father always said you were brilliant. In a few years, that research Kestler is doing will be worth a bundle.''

That's what everyone kept telling her.

''Your 'kind, considerate husband' didn't fake his references with Zuckerman's for nothing, you know. He looked around for a plum and your father dropped Patterson right into his greedy little hands.''

Greg's words poked further holes in her crumbling wall of self-esteem. Was Greg right? Had she and her father been so blinded by their own needs that they hadn't seen Paul for what he really was?

"I own Patterson," she reminded him.

"Uh-huh. And he married *you*. How long before expansion forces you to place a block of stock on the open market?"

The issue had already been raised. The new process required an infusion of capital soon. Paul had been pushing them to go public for over a month now. Was Greg right? Had her judgments become completely unreliable?

Greg kneaded his right thigh, his strong hands massaging the skin beneath his twill slacks. McKella seized on that to avoid the direction her thoughts were taking.

"Did the doctor look at your leg?"

Immediately, his hand withdrew. "No."

"Why not?"

"I didn't hurt my leg."

She tipped her head to one side in disbelief.

"It's an old injury," he explained wearily.

"Like your other scars?"

"Yeah."

"Do you mind if I ask how you got them?"

He sighed and shut his eyes again. "I was in a car accident as a teenager."

The front door swung open and the cabby slid inside before she could pursue the topic. "We can get around on the right, now. They say the road is clear the rest of the way. I should have you back at your hotel in a few minutes."

The driver was as good his word, and he'd been right about the electricity. Other than emergency lights, the hotel didn't have any. Greg reeled when he stepped from the cab, and McKella had to half support him up the three flights of stairs to his room.

Her wet clothes chafed her skin, and she was exhausted. She wanted to get Greg situated so she could return to her own room and slip into something dry and comfortable.

He used the bathroom while she prowled his bedroom. As he came out, he swayed. "Want me to help you undress?" she asked, hurrying to his side.

He attempted a leer—without success. "Maybe later. I can manage."

"Right. I can see that."

Masculine pride was such a fragile thing.

McKella decided to use the facilities rather than to watch him struggle with his shoes. Greg was under the covers on the king-size bed by the time she came out. A pile of damp clothing littered the floor. His bare arms and a view of the top of his chest made her wonder if he wore anything at all beneath that sheet and blanket.

"There's a sweatshirt in the closet that should work as a nightgown," he told her groggily.

"What are you talking about? I don't need a nightgown. I'm going to my—"

"No, you aren't." All trace of weakness left his voice. With effort he lifted himself on an elbow.

"I beg your pardon?"

"You don't have to beg, you just have to stay here."

"Don't worry, I'll be back, Greg. Get some rest." She started for the door.

He sat all the way up with a groan of pain that stopped her in her tracks. The sheet dropped. Greg was bare to the waist.

"Go out that door and I'll go after you stark naked."

So much for wondering what he wore. "You wouldn't dare."

He flung back the covers and swung his feet over the side. She immediately averted her gaze, fixing it on his obstinate face. "Get back in bed."

"Release the doorknob."

"What's wrong with you?"

"I could ask you the same question, but I'm too tired for games right now, McKella. We don't know where your husband is. Do you really want to find yourself facing him alone right now?"

Air caught in her throat. "He wouldn't— You don't think— Why would he go to my room?"

"Where else can he go?"

"We should call Constable Freer."

"No phones, remember?"

"I could go downstairs and get Security."

"You could," he agreed. "But someone might get hurt. Hotel security isn't any match for a desperate man. If he's upstairs waiting for you, let him wait. Frankly, I'm so tired I don't care where he is or what he's doing. Are you so anxious to have him arrested that it can't wait until we've had some rest?"

Of course she didn't want Paul arrested. At least not until she talked to him. It was desperately hard to think. Even harder to keep her eyes where they belonged. They strayed, and she caught a glimpse of white. "You're wearing briefs!"

A smile curved his lips. "You peeked."

She was thankful for the dimness of the room, which she hoped would hide the blush she knew stained her cheeks.

"Greg—"

"McKella, he can wait 'til morning. And I promise

you, no matter how badly I want you, if you stripped for me right now, I probably wouldn't be able to do anything but savor the memory. I'm more asleep than awake. Come to bed.''

"I'm not sleeping with you."

He held up a hand in protest. "It's a big bed. I promise, that's all we'll do. I'll stay under the blanket on my side, and you can take the comforter.'' His voice dropped. "Please. I need to know you're safe.''

If he hadn't added that last, she could have ignored him. Maybe.

She released the doorknob. She would lie down until he fell asleep—which should take about three seconds given his present condition, she decided. Then she could go downstairs and get someone from Security to check her room. If only the idea of climbing into bed with Greg wasn't doing such strange things to her nervous system...

"The sweatshirt's in the closet?'' she asked.

"Hanging up.''

Why did this feel like such a dangerous mistake? "I want a quick shower first.'' Maybe if she dallied in the bathroom, he'd fall asleep and never notice she was gone.

"Promise you won't leave?''

Blast the man. "Don't you trust me?''

The corners of his mouth quirked as he tried to smile again. "With my life.'' He slid back under the sheet and blanket and closed his eyes.

The solemn way that he uttered those words made mincemeat of her resolve. McKella went to the closet, found the black sweatshirt and reentered the bathroom. The sweatshirt, she soon discovered, while plenty roomy and smelling tantalizingly of Greg's spicy aftershave, did little more than cover her lower extremities.

There was something naughty and intimate about the feel of the nubby material against her bare skin. Self-conscious, she stepped back into the bedroom. Greg didn't move. He was on his side facing her and appeared to be sound asleep.

She studied his strong profile, unsettled by emotions she didn't want to examine too closely. She could leave right now and he'd be none the wiser. But she found she couldn't do it. She had all but promised to stay.

As silently and as carefully as she could, she slid under the comforter on the far side of the bed.

"'Night 'Kella."

His drowsy voice warmed the dark room.

"Go to sleep, Greg." She closed her own eyes, knowing that falling to sleep would be a difficult chore for her, despite the exhaustion slowly robbing her of strength. She was entirely too aware of the man on the other side of the bed.

GREG HEARD THE FIRM RAP on the door and hurried to answer before McKella woke up. He toweled away the last vestiges of shaving cream as he unlatched the door and swung it open. The now-familiar lanky police detective stood on the other side, hand raised to knock again.

"Ah, you are here."

Greg moved to block Freer when he would have entered the room, but it was too late. McKella called out in sleepy confusion.

"Good. Mrs. Dinsmore is here as well."

"Uh, yeah. Could you come back in a few—"

"Who is it, Greg?"

McKella arrived at his side, looking rumpled and sleepy and sexy as hell in his sweatshirt.

Resigned to the inevitable, Greg expelled a long breath. "Constable Freer."

"Oh." Abruptly, her eyes grew round. "Oh, blast."

"Yeah. I'd say that sums it up nicely. Your clothes are mostly dry now."

Pink tinged her cheeks. She looked past Greg to the man who watched the scene with quiet interest.

"Let him in, Greg. If you gentlemen will excuse me while I dress? This isn't what it looks like." She started for the bathroom and stopped, turning to Greg. "I need coffee. I don't suppose we have electricity yet?"

"Sorry." He stepped back and motioned the detective inside. The man took in the rumpled bed and the pile of clothing without so much as a raised eyebrow.

"She's right, you know. This *isn't* what it looks like. We shared a bed, but not each other," Greg told him.

"I see."

"I doubt it." Greg headed for the closet and yanked out his last polo shirt. Gently, he pulled the green knit over his head, wincing when he brushed the tender skin near the crown. If he didn't have such a thick skull, he'd be dead right now.

"How *is* your head, Mr. Wyman?"

Freer didn't overlook much. No doubt he'd already seen the full doctor's report. "It hurts like hell, thank you. What time is it anyhow? My watch stopped."

"Ten past three."

Amazed, Greg strode across the room to pull back the heavy drapes. The dismal, rainy view let in little additional light.

"You and Mrs. Dinsmore had an eventful evening."

He faced the detective, wondering what the man was thinking. "You could say that."

"And Mr. Dinsmore was also present?"

"For a little while. Fortunately, he disappeared along with the tornado. With any luck, he's halfway across the ocean by now."

The officer cocked his head. Greg would have sworn that he saw a sparkle of amusement whisk across the man's obsidian eyes.

"I gather you do not know his whereabouts at the present time?"

"Not a clue."

"You went to the cottage to meet him?"

"No," McKella stated from the bathroom doorway, "I did. Greg just went along for the ride."

Her blouse and slacks were hopelessly wrinkled. There was a tear at one knee, while the other was badly stained. Yet her hair was combed, drifting around her flushed face. Adorable was probably not the image she wanted to present, but that was just how she looked to Greg.

"You did not think to tell me of your plans?" Freer asked her.

"I thought about it, but I discarded the idea." She raised her chin.

McKella didn't need a power outfit to don her professional persona, Greg decided. Too bad she hadn't wanted to take over Patterson Opticals. She could have done the job. She was quite capable of holding her own right now, despite her rumpled appearance and the compromising situation.

"I needed to speak with Paul first," she told Freer, "to find out what is going on."

"And were you successful?"

She shook her head, a bleak expression settling over her features. "The tornado intervened."

"Really? You were inside for an hour and seventeen minutes before the tornado struck."

"You were watching us?" Greg asked.

"One of my men drove your cab."

Sucker-punched again, he thought. "Well, why the hell didn't he *do* something?"

Freer scratched absently at his head. "About what, Mr. Wyman? I assure you, halting tornados is not in his job description. His job was to observe and report. I am afraid he had a slight mishap after he dropped the two of you off. The storm, you understand."

"Is he all right?" McKella asked quickly.

"Quite all right, thank you. The car, I am afraid, suffered a fate similar to your cottage."

Greg sat down in the chair to pull on his still uncomfortably wet shoes. "Have you found her husband yet?"

"I am afraid not. If Mrs. Dinsmore—McKella—hadn't been so insistent that he was in the rubble last night, we would not have known he had been there at all."

She plopped down on the edge of the bed. "He only arrived a few minutes before the tornado."

Greg shook his head. "He was there all along, 'Kella."

"Where? We checked the house."

"I never checked the balconies. He must have waited outside while I searched the upstairs."

McKella looked pained. "I don't understand any of this."

The officer looked pointedly from one to the other of them, then at the large bed. "Nor do I."

"McKella slept on top of the sheets," Greg was quick to defend. "I slept under them. I was afraid to let her go back to her room alone and I couldn't make it that far."

"Afraid?"

Greg met the other man's bland expression. "Afraid her husband would show up. Afraid you'd have another dead body on your hands."

"You still believe her husband will kill her, Mr. Wyman?"

"Someone tried to. Remember the café?"

McKella bristled. "That truck killed the woman who was rooming with Betty Jane."

"And would have killed us if we hadn't gotten out of the way," Greg retorted.

"The lorry could have been directed at any one of you. Or all three," Freer pointed out calmly.

Greg pinched the bridge of his nose, wishing his headache would settle to a dull throb.

"Interesting that you mentioned the accident," Freer continued. "Before the telephone lines were disrupted, I received some information."

Greg braced himself for what he knew was coming.

"Eleanor Miller Dinsmore Beauchamp appears to have been married to Paul Dinsmore as well."

Stunned, McKella stared at the officer while her heart pounded against her chest.

"You were not aware of this fact?" Freer asked.

"No." She turned toward Greg in pain and accusation. He'd known. She was sure of it when his eyes met hers.

"Were you aware your husband has a juvenile record?" Freer wanted to know.

McKella didn't even glance at the policeman, but her

fingers curled at her sides as she remembered Greg had told her about the warehouse. He hadn't lied about that. Maybe everything else he'd told her had been the truth as well.

"Paul was a criminal?"

"Misdemeanors," Freer told her. "Fistfights, disturbing the peace, traffic violations. He was questioned about several thefts, but no charges were ever brought." Freer paused. "Not even when Paul Dinsmore, his friend Jason McConnel, and McConnel's younger brother Brendon—or BG as he was known—were questioned in the death of McConnel's father."

Her body absorbed the words like blows. "No," she whispered. She shook her head in groggy negation. Greg's impassive stare never left her face. He had known all this and yet he hadn't told her.

Because he was Jason McConnel?

"According to the report," Freer continued, "the three young men were the scourge of their small town. Trouble followed them wherever they went."

No expression showed on Greg's face or in his cloudy blue-green eyes. McKella turned away.

"Is this what Eric Henning discovered?" she asked the officer.

"That is, of course, possible," Freer conceded. "I thought perhaps you knew about your husband's past."

Her chin came up. "No. It's becoming clear to me that I know absolutely nothing at all about my husband. What I thought I knew seems to consist of lies. Was Paul divorced from either woman?"

The question startled the policeman. "Do you have reason to question this?"

She sensed Greg tense as he waited for her reply, but she didn't glance in his direction.

"Given everything else you're discovering about his past, nothing would surprise me. Paul told me Betty Jane had approached him to say their divorce wasn't final. He claimed she wanted money."

McKella couldn't quite bring herself to expose the things Greg had told her, despite her certainty that he had lied to her—at least by omission.

"You did not mention this before," Freer chided.

"I felt I owed my husband my loyalty before. Now…" She shrugged. "It will simplify my divorce proceedings if we aren't legally married." She only hoped the pain building inside her didn't show. She had worried about turning into a wuss. Instead, she should have worried about being a gullible fool.

"Indeed." Freer rubbed thoughtfully at the back of his head, his eyes moving from one to the other. "It cannot be coincidence that all of you are on Bermuda at this time."

"Agreed," McKella told him.

The officer cocked his head and waited, looking from one face to the other. Greg remained mute.

"Do you have anything to add, Mr. Wyman?" he asked after a moment.

"No, sir."

"You know that we will find a connection if it exists. Far better for you to tell me now."

"Sorry. I can't tell you anything."

"We are a small police force, Mr. Wyman, but we are not stupid."

"No, sir. I'd say you are far from that."

The officer inclined his head, accepting the faint praise. Then he inhaled and released the air on a long sigh. "At the moment, Mr. Wyman, I can find nothing to tie you to Mr. Dinsmore or the two dead women."

"Good. I don't fancy being a suspect in a situation like this one."

"Ah, but you are. I am afraid until we get to the bottom of things, your proximity to these events leaves me no choice but to consider both of you suspects in the murder of Betty Jane Dinsmore."

"What? Why?" McKella demanded. "We were sitting in the café. There's no way we could have killed that poor woman."

Greg stepped forward. She felt his solid presence inches from her back.

"McKella's actions should be easy enough to trace from the time her plane landed," he said.

"I don't need you to defend me, Greg," she said without turning around. She sensed his hurt at her rebuke, but continued. "As the constable said, his officers are far from stupid."

"Indeed."

"Fine," Greg agreed quietly. "I'm afraid proving my actions will take more effort, but I'm sure at least one of the shopkeepers will remember me. I spent rather lavishly in a couple of the menswear shops here in St. George's. In fact, I have the receipts in my wallet. With any luck, one or two will have time-and-date stamps on them."

McKella's heart pounded, as he retrieved his wallet and sorted through the damp contents. Whatever reason Greg had for keeping information from her, she was certain he hadn't murdered anyone.

"Why would either one of us kill Betty Jane?" she asked in what she hoped was a reasonable tone of voice.

"Why, indeed?" Freer glanced meaningfully at the

bed, and McKella knew she blushed. Greg clenched his teeth.

"I will obtain more information once the trunk lines are restored," Freer told them. "For now, I request that the two of you remain available for further questions."

At least he wasn't going to arrest them.

Freer accompanied them down the hall to McKella's room. She left the two men standing there talking while she went in to change clothing.

As she pulled on a jumpsuit, she remembered that Greg had used Eleanor's maiden name when he confronted Paul in the cottage. If he was really Jason McConnel, as she suspected, he must know a lot about her husband. Hadn't the constable said the two men had been friends?

Her ring snagged on the soft material of her outfit. If Greg was telling her the truth, she wasn't legally married to Paul at all. The ring's diamond winked in the light as if to mock her.

A hollow emptiness filled her. What else did Greg know that he hadn't told her? And why was he hiding his own past?

As Greg Wyman, he had a solid reputation in the business world. Obviously, the last thing he would want would be to have a disreputable past come to light. Still, she refused to believe he'd resort to murder to protect his reputation.

She made a wry face in the mirror. Her judgment of people had proved worthless. Both Greg and Paul had suckered her from the outset. There was no consolation in the knowledge that her father had been just as easily deceived.

Someone tapped on the door. "McKella? You okay?"

No. She might never feel okay again.

"Coming." She smoothed the one-piece jumpsuit over her hips, wishing she hadn't chosen such provocative outfits to wear for her new husband. She no longer wondered why Paul hadn't taken her to bed. Now she was simply grateful.

McKella drew back her shoulders and straightened her spine. Maybe she'd been a fool, but she wasn't stupid. She hadn't loved Paul; she had *liked* him. And if he *had* killed Betty Jane, she would help put him in jail where he belonged. She removed her rings and slid them into the pocket of her jumpsuit.

Greg moved away from the wall with a small grimace when McKella opened the door. "You look like you went ten rounds and lost," she told him. The words were defensive, because while his face appeared bruised and battered, Greg still managed to look incredibly sexy.

"Thanks," he drawled. His gaze roamed her body. "You, on the other hand, were worth the wait."

His softly spoken words feathered her like a caress, leaving her immediately vulnerable. She refused to acknowledge the feminine reaction his intent expression stirred to life.

"Let's go to Hamilton," he suggested before she could summon a suitable response.

"Why?"

He tipped his head, a smile hovering at the corners of his lips. "They have electricity now. Hot coffee? Scones? Maybe a nice thick juicy hamburger?"

"You think you can bribe me?" Even suspecting what she did, it was hard to resist that boyish expression on his face. Her stomach rumbled, and his smile widened at the sound.

"Sounds like it. At least part of you wants to go with me."

Ha. More than part of her wanted to go with him, she acknowledged. Once a fool, always a fool? McKella pulled her windbreaker around her like a shield.

"What about Constable Freer?"

"He can buy his own hamburger."

"Greg—"

"Freer left. He's the one who suggested we go to Hamilton. Honest. He said he'd see us later."

"Okay, but I—"

"Have a lot of questions. I know." His eyes held a trace of sorrow that erased her exasperation. "Can the answers wait until after we eat?"

"Paul wouldn't answer my questions, either."

His expression hardened and his voice could have sliced through concrete. "Ask me anything you want, but don't ever lump me together with your husband."

She was stunned by the depth of his anger. "You really hate him."

"That's a fair assessment."

"Why?"

His gaze roved the corridor. A maid was starting toward them from the far end of the hall. "Do you really want to stand out here and discuss this right now, McKella?"

Part of her did. The need to understand was strong. But he was right, this was hardly the place for this discussion.

"I didn't kill Betty Jane, McKella," he said softly.

She met his solemn gaze and resisted an impulse to reach out and touch him. "I know that."

"You do?"

McKella nodded. "You accused Paul last night, remember? You were too furious to be faking."

Some of the tension left his stance. "Thanks. I think. I still believe he killed her. He's capable, and he has a motive."

"Don't you?"

"No."

She tipped her head in disbelief.

"I'm no saint, McKella. I'd kill if I had to protect myself or someone I cared about, but Betty Jane was no threat to me." Sincerity underscored his words.

Greg watched her openly. Slowly, he extended his hand. She steeled her heart and her fears and accepted his touch.

At a noisy restaurant in the middle of downtown Hamilton they ate fish chowder and finger foods. Conversation about the storm's devastation filled the room.

McKella listened to Greg's whiskey-soft voice as she prompted him to tell her about building a successful business. The depth and scope of his knowledge astounded her.

"No wonder you can take a floundering firm and rebuild. You love a challenge, don't you?"

"Guilty as charged."

"And you aren't afraid to try innovative techniques. You know, you're exactly the sort of CEO my father was looking for when he hired Paul."

And that reminder brought their conversation to a crashing halt. Like any well-trained waiter, theirs arrived at that moment to deliver coffee and impossibly large slices of Key lime pie.

In the silence, McKella studied Greg's face. Where Paul was movie-star handsome, Greg's features were more rugged—more "lived in." And he possessed an inner strength that was lacking in most people of her acquaintance.

"Have I got something on my chin?" he asked.

She smiled. "No."

"Then what's that look for?"

She raised her cup quickly to avert a blush. "Never mind."

"Oh? I think I like the sound of that."

"What does *that* mean?" She held the cup without taking a sip.

"It means I like the way you were looking at me."

She lowered the cup to its saucer with a definite clink. At the moment, his eyes were more green than blue, and he was studying her with a predatory look.

"If I ask you some questions, will you tell me the truth?" she asked quickly.

Her words had the desired effect. Instantly, his expression sobered. "I've never lied to you, McKella."

"Except by omission?"

He shifted, scanning the room before answering her. "Except by omission," he agreed.

"Why are you being so secretive, Greg? What else do you know about Paul that I should know?"

He returned her stare, his eyes abruptly shadowed. "I'd rather answer what I can where only the seagulls are close enough to overhear. Are you finished eating?"

She looked down at her mostly untouched pie, knowing that she couldn't eat another bite. "Yes."

"Let's get out of here."

McKella waited, while Greg paid the bill and then led her to a small park overlooking the wharf. With a light drizzle stinging their faces, they walked along the muddy ground, skirting storm debris. Greg guided her around a huge, broken tree limb and paused by a weathered bench, where he could stare out over the sullen water.

"When I knew him," Greg began without warning, "your husband lived on the wrong side of town with his brother and an abusive, alcoholic father."

McKella had to strain to hear his low words, a forbidding contrast to his turbulent expression.

"He learned early to use his looks and charm to talk his way out of trouble," Greg continued. "And he was *always* in trouble."

He glanced at her and back out at the water. "Women were drawn to his looks and his bad-boy image. He used them without a qualm. Betty Jane, for example, probably helped him learn enough to fake a work history in someone else's computer files."

"You think Paul falsified Zuckerman's employment records?"

"I'd bet on it. It isn't that hard to do if you know how."

"Do you?"

He turned to look at her. "Yes."

The simple answer surprised her as much as his enigmatic expression.

"I told you I was no saint."

No, he was more devil than saint, she thought. The bad-boy image fit him more easily than it did Paul.

She brought her wayward thoughts into line. "Have you ever done that? Faked a background, I mean?"

"Yes. Once."

"Oh." Questions crowded her mind, but along with them came some suggested answers. If he was Jason McConnel, he'd created the Greg Wyman persona. And as much as she wanted to learn everything there was to know about him, that would have to wait. "Did you know the woman who was killed outside the café?"

"Yes." He was quiet for a long time, watching the waves slap against the dock. "I didn't recognize her at first. She was barely eighteen the last time I saw her. I didn't know she'd married him." A dark emotion lurked beneath those words.

McKella resisted an impulse to ask him how well he'd known the eighteen-year-old woman. "She must have been coming to see *you* at the café," she suggested instead.

Greg shook his head. "No. She never even looked at me. I'm sure she was heading for you. She was probably coming to warn you about him."

Him. Greg had never once called Paul by name. "Possible, I guess, but how would she know who I was?"

His shoulders lifted and fell quickly. "Like me, Eleanor must have seen the ads and called Betty Jane. My guess is they caught an earlier flight and were waiting for you at the airport. When the two of you split up, Eleanor must have followed you, while Betty Jane went to talk with your husband."

Greg's words made a scary sort of sense. People *had* been watching her argue with Paul at the airport, but she didn't remember noticing anyone in particular. And really, what did it matter? Unless...

"You think Paul was driving that truck?"

Greg hesitated so long that she thought he wasn't going to answer. When he turned to face her again, his expression was stony.

"Yeah. I do."

The hollow coldness seeped back into her chest. McKella shook her head. "I don't believe it. How would Paul have had time to steal a truck *and* find me at that café?''

His hands balled at his sides. "I don't know, but who else would want you dead?''

"No one.''

He watched her without saying another word.

"You never call him by name,'' she said slowly. "Why don't you ever refer to Paul by name?''

"Because Paul Dinsmore is dead, McKella. He died fifteen years ago.''

Chapter Seven

"What are you talking about?" McKella demanded. Blood pounded behind her eyes, making her light-headed. Groping for the back of the bench in front of her, she stared at Greg. Eric Henning's phone message echoed in her mind. *"It's about your husband...not one of his references has ever met the guy...there are lots of possible explanations..."*

Greg reached for her in concern. "You aren't going to faint, are you?"

She stepped away from his touch, forcing air from her tortured lungs, only then realizing she'd been holding her breath.

"I'm not going to faint."

"I shouldn't have sprung that on you. I'm sorry."

"Sorry?" She shook her head, welcoming the surge of anger that pulsed through her. "Sorry doesn't cut it, you worm. You've played mind games with me from the start, dropping bits and pieces of information, never explaining, but always so solicitous."

"McKella—"

She jerked her arm from his reaching fingers. "Don't touch me. I want explanations. Complete explanations.

If Paul Dinsmore is dead, then who did I marry?'' Her voice shook with fury.

For the first time in her life, she wanted to strike another person.

''And don't you dare...don't you *dare* tell me you can't explain. So help me, I'll go right to Constable Freer and tell him to arrest you for withholding information.''

Greg dropped one hand to his side. With the other, he wiped at the raindrops misting his eyes. ''I told you, I was intrigued by the puzzle those ads presented because I knew your husband. I just didn't tell you I knew he'd been involved in a fatal car crash fifteen years ago.''

''Why not?'' she demanded. ''How do you know so much about Paul?''

They stared at one another over the back of the bench.

''Because I was there the night he died.''

Stunned by the emotionless words, McKella's heart began to pound as though she'd been running. She remembered the extensive scarring on Greg's body, the signs of plastic surgery on his face. Yes, she believed him.

''When I saw the first ad,'' he said softly, ''his name came as a shock. Then I decided it must be another Paul Dinsmore. I should have ignored the damn thing, but I kept remembering that murder contract. Anyone using Paul's identity was in danger.''

''You were going to warn him?'' McKella wrapped her arms around her body.

Greg shrugged. ''At first I was just curious.''

''Until you realized who Paul was,'' she concluded. He didn't deny her charge.

"You didn't like my husband."

"You're right. I didn't."

McKella inhaled sharply. She decided to let that pass in favor of a more pressing question. "If Paul isn't Paul, then who is he?"

Greg shoved his hands in his pockets and rocked back on his heels. "Jason McConnel."

The words slammed into her, robbing her of breath for a moment. "Paul's friend?"

"They were never friends," he said fiercely.

"But, I thought you…" She couldn't finish the sentence, but she didn't have to.

His jaw clenched. "You thought I was Jason."

"Well…yes. It seemed…possible."

Greg muttered something and turned back to the water, his back stiff with anger.

"The constable mentioned McConnel. He was the man whose father died under questionable circumstances."

"They were questionable all right," he snarled. "I always suspected Jason killed him."

Stunned by his statement, McKella stared at him. "You don't mean that."

The very softness of his answer was chilling. "Want to bet? Supposedly, the old man fell into Miller's pond coming home one night. I guess it could have happened that way. Ned McConnel was a mean son of a bitch when he was drunk and, toward the end, he was always drunk."

"You knew him," she stated, trying to put the facts together. It was easier than trying to deal with the possibility that the man she had married was not only a complete fraud, but might also have killed his own father.

Greg didn't respond right away. He stared out over the restless water. "I knew all of them. Jason and the real Paul Dinsmore grew up in the same part of town." His low voice vibrated with restrained emotion.

"It wasn't a nice part of town and they weren't nice young men." He turned, not quite facing her but no longer in profile. His eyes stared at the landscape, but McKella knew he was seeing something quite different. She wished she could stop his flow of memories, but she needed to learn the truth, and she suspected he needed to tell it.

"Where Jason wielded his charming lies like weapons, Paul was a typical rebellious teen. His habitual anger and stiff-necked pride made it easy for Jason to blame him whenever things went wrong."

Moisture trickled inside her collar. McKella ignored the unpleasant sensation, and focused on Greg.

"Jason had a younger brother, BG. When Paul left town right after graduation, Jason had to do the same, or find someone new to start blaming for his actions. BG wouldn't have been as easy to target as Paul. BG was younger, bigger and a lot brighter. He wouldn't have stood by in silence when he was accused of something he hadn't done."

"Like Paul did?"

"Yeah. Paul dated Eleanor a couple of times, but her father put a stop to it. The old man must have had kittens when Jason married her. I'm guessing Jason used her to get enough money to start life in the fast lane. Her father owned a box company, the biggest employer in town. He would have paid plenty to get rid of an unwanted son-in-law."

"Wait a minute," McKella interrupted. "The constable said Eleanor married Paul Dinsmore, not Jason McConnel.''

''I know what he said.'' Greg faced her, his features calm once more. ''That had me stumped too, but I'm betting Jason used Paul's name instead of his own on the marriage certificate. Remember, he liked to blame Paul for everything. Even his marriages, apparently.''

''But that wouldn't be legal.''

Greg uttered a harsh laugh. ''That's probably why he did it. It would be interesting to know if her daddy got the marriage annulled before or after Jason skipped town.''

''But could Paul...I mean, Jason...I mean...how could he get away with signing someone else's name? Wouldn't the judge or someone notice the discrepancy?''

Greg shrugged and jammed his hands down into the pockets of his pants. ''Who knows? All I can tell you for certain is that the real Paul Dinsmore never married Eleanor. Since Eleanor was here on the island, it's a cinch your Paul is the one she married.''

Her thoughts whirled, but she seized one from the chaos. ''What happened to Jason's brother?''

Greg flashed her an approving look. ''BG was a minor. With his parents dead and Paul gone, social services stepped in.''

''BG.'' She gripped the back of the bench. Greg wasn't Jason, he was Jason's brother! ''Did the G stand for Gregory?''

Greg tensed, but not because of her question. His gaze had locked on something past her shoulder. McKella twisted and saw a policeman hurrying in their direction.

''Now what?'' Greg muttered.

"Mrs. Dinsmore?" the man called out.

McKella nodded reluctantly.

"Constable Freer needs to see you right away, miss."

Her stomach lurched in foreboding. "They found Paul?"

"I couldn't say, miss. If you and Mr. Wyman will come this way, I have a car waiting."

Intensely frustrated at the interruption, but hoping answers were finally at hand, she pinned Greg with a look. "We'll finish this conversation later."

His eyes crinkled at the corners as he took her arm. "I wouldn't have it any other way."

Half an hour later, he still held her arm, but this time in a gesture of comfort as she sat stiffly in a hard-backed chair facing the constable.

"Did they tell you my father's condition?" she demanded of the man.

Freer shook his head. "I am sorry. This is the fax that came through." He slid a paper across the desk. Neither McKella nor Greg made any move to touch the white sheet. The constable nodded sympathetically. "There was an accident at Patterson Opticals. Your father was taken to a local hospital. I have made arrangements to clear you through customs immediately." He looked at Greg. "There is only one seat available on this flight."

Greg nodded his understanding and squeezed McKella's cold hand. "Do you want to wait until I can go with you?"

"Mrs. Dinsmore," Freer interrupted, "the decision, of course, is yours, but you must leave now if you wish to make the flight. They will not hold the plane. My officer is standing by to drive you to the airport. A replacement credit card will be waiting for you there.''

McKella stood immediately. ''Thank you.''

Freer also stood. ''Is there anything further I may do to be of help?''

''No. Thank you.'' Pain gilded her eyes as she turned away. ''Greg, could you...would you mind seeing to my belongings?''

''I'll take care of it.'' He stroked the back of her hand, and she clasped his fingers, giving them a quick squeeze. ''Go ahead. I'll catch a later flight and catch up with you in Louisville.''

''You don't have to do that,'' she protested.

''Yes,'' he told her. ''I do. We never finished our conversation, remember?''

McKella laid her hand on his arm and he saw the fine tremor that rocked her fingers. ''Thank you. And again, thank you, Constable.''

''Have a safe flight,'' Freer offered.

Giving him a sad little smile, she turned toward the door.

''I'll see you in a few hours,'' Greg promised. ''And try not to worry. Things will work out. Your dad is tough, McKella.''

Her spine straightened. ''Yes, he is,'' she said without a backward glance. ''It's a family trait.''

Greg found a reluctant smile playing at the corner of his lips. He saw his own admiration reflected in Freer's expression before the man's official mask settled back into place. As McKella disappeared, the officer resumed his seat, indicating with a nod that Greg should do the same.

''What about her missing husband?'' Greg asked.

Freer leaned back in his chair, the pen in his hand

tapping against the frayed blotter on his desk. The tapping showed more emotion than the policeman had displayed to date.

"I regret to say we believe he left the island this morning. Due to a mix-up, I was not informed until after the plane had reached its destination."

Greg immediately understood the man's agitation. Freer was left holding no suspects, but with two dead bodies.

"Wasn't the airport alerted not to let him off the island?"

The other man's lips pursed as though he'd bitten into a lemon. "He used your ticket and identification. Somehow, the order restricting your travel was overlooked and there is a strong resemblance between you and Mr. Dinsmore. Things were chaotic due to the storm. A new employee was on duty..." His shoulders inched upward in a small shrug.

Greg wasn't deceived. The new employee was probably looking for another line of work at the moment.

"Police in the States have been informed," Freer added. "Mr. Dinsmore will be apprehended and returned to Bermuda to stand charges."

The officer had more faith than Greg did. "So where does that leave me?"

Freer dropped the pen and held his gaze. "Is there anything you wish to tell me about your participation in these events?"

For a brief instant, Greg wished he dared confide in the man. He liked Freer. Respected him.

Greg shook his head.

"You understand, you will need to return here?"

Greg nodded. "Unlike her husband, I don't plan to disappear."

"Good. I am sorry about McKella's father. I hope he will recover." He stood, extending his hand. Greg felt a pang of guilt as he clasped it.

"There are some forms you will need to fill out first, but another flight leaves in an hour."

"I'll be on it."

"Indeed."

Greg left, wishing there was something he could say beyond the simple thank-you. Freer could have made the situation difficult. Instead, Greg was free to pursue McKella.

FIRST HER PLANE WAS DELAYED, then McKella ended up in a hideous traffic jam. By the time she reached the hospital she discovered she would have to wait almost an hour to see her father. Tired and anxious, she found a sympathetic charge nurse who gave her the name of the attending physician and a brief rundown on her father's condition.

During an apparent heart attack, he'd fallen and struck his head against a desk. He was in a coma.

Heartsick, McKella went in search of a telephone. As she passed the door to the stairwell, it banged opened. A flurry of movement caused her to turn in that direction, but something white descended forcefully to cover her head and face. Arms pinned her, dragging her backward into the stairwell.

McKella struggled wildly, desperate to free her arms and face. The white material was heavy—suffocating. She kicked backward and connected with a shin, eliciting a low grunt of pain. The metal stair rail bumped hard against her hip. Her captor added weight to the momentum. He was trying to push her over the railing!

Fear lent new impetus to her struggle. She twisted

free, stumbling away from the rail. At the same instant, from somewhere overhead came a masculine shout. As McKella battled to pull the heavy material from her head, a hard shove sent her flying backwards.

She clawed for a handhold, but she found only empty air. Her hip scraped the metal railing as she plunged backward down the concrete stairs.

GREG SPOTTED THE KNOT of people near the end of the hall as soon as he stepped from the elevator. He sprinted forward, heart thundering in his chest. He heard McKella's voice before he reached her.

"I don't want X rays. I'm fine, just bruised."

Greg shouldered his way past the onlookers. Two security men helped McKella into the hall. Her eyes lit in a welcome that would have warmed him at any other time.

"Greg!"

"What's it been," he asked, coming to a halt inches away, "six hours? How can one woman get in so much trouble in such a short space of time?"

Her chin lifted, her eyes flashed, then her lips parted in a wobbly smile. "Practice," she told him.

He opened his arms and enfolded her against his chest. Her body quaked as reaction set in. He fixed the security men with a glare. "What happened?"

"Somebody tried to shove her down the stairwell," the smaller of the two men answered.

"Yeah, and if Jim here hadn't spotted what was happening and yelled, she'd have been killed instead of falling down half a flight of steps."

"Scared the hell outta me," Jim agreed.

"I'm fine," she insisted. Her voice was muffled against Greg's damp jacket as she tried to pull away.

Greg didn't let her go. He wasn't sure he could, with the fear clawing his belly. He cupped the back of her head, feeling for lumps.

She could have been killed.

"Greg, it's okay," McKella told him. She leaned back to look up at him.

"Have the police been called?" he demanded.

"They're on their way," the one called Jim assured him.

"Did you get a look at him?"

"Not really. I was coming down from Five when I heard the scuffle." He nodded at McKella. "The guy had a hood or something over his own head, so I never got any kind of look at him. Hell, I don't even know if it was a him or a her. It all happened pretty fast."

"Greg, I'm fine," she told him again.

He kissed the top of her head. "Let them take you downstairs to be checked. Please, McKella." He stared down the mutiny in her eyes. "I need to know you're okay."

"I'm just a little bruised and shaken."

"Prove it."

"I'm not going to miss the visiting hour with my father," she challenged.

"You won't," he promised recklessly.

McKella surrendered and allowed him to help her to the elevator. She was adamant in her refusal of a gurney or a wheelchair, and by then, the police had arrived in the form of a young, brusque officer who asked questions of her and the security men all the way to the emergency room.

Within thirty minutes, she had charmed, cowed or intimidated everyone around her. Greg was impressed. He also throbbed with unresolved rage.

The doctor agreed she was only bruised, and McKella bullied her way back upstairs in time for the visiting hour with her father. A nurse invited McKella in past the double doors and pointed Greg in the direction of the waiting room.

He had only been sitting there a short time when a dapper man hurried down the corridor. After a brief discussion with the nurse, the man turned and headed for the area where Greg sat.

Though Greg had never met Larry Patterson, he recognized McKella's uncle right away. "Mr. Patterson?"

Cold blue eyes surveyed him, taking in the unzipped jacket and casual shirt and pants he hadn't bothered to change before leaving Bermuda.

"Yes?"

"I'm Greg Wyman, a friend of McKella's." He waited to see if his name would ring any bells, but apparently Larry Patterson didn't remember the name of the man who had discovered his fraudulent activities.

The handshake was firm, but brief. "The nurse said she was here. Where's Paul?"

"McKella's husband disappeared shortly after they arrived in Bermuda."

"Disappeared?"

"Yes, sir. He's wanted for questioning by the Bermuda police."

"Is this some sort of joke, young man?"

It would be easy to dislike this pompous man, Greg decided, but he was McKella's uncle, and she was loyal to her friends and family.

"Not at all, Mr. Patterson. I'm surprised the police haven't been in contact with you by now."

"I've been out at the plant. We had an accident there last night."

"Yes, sir. Your brother's heart attack."

"Yes, well, that and the fire have made for a busy several hours."

"I wasn't aware there had been a fire."

Larry Patterson frowned. "No reason you should. One of the labs caught fire. That's how they found Henry. He was lying in the foyer of the executive offices. Must have had a heart attack when the alarm went off."

"I thought McKella's father was retired."

"He is."

"Then what was he doing at the office?"

Frost deepened his glare but amazingly, Patterson chose to respond. "No one knows," he said tersely.

"How did the fire start?"

"I've no idea. The fire department's looking into it. Probably an electrical short or something. Fortunately, the building was empty except for the night watchman who escaped without harm, and, of course, Henry."

"Uh-huh." A fire with inexplicable origins, and a heart attack coupled with a head injury. Greg would take bets the blow had come before the attack. He'd also take bets that the lab that had caught fire was the one used by their prized research chemist.

"What's all this about Paul and the police?" Larry demanded.

As Greg briefly explained, he realized that there was no way McKella's husband could be responsible for the fire or her father's injury. He hadn't left Bermuda until this morning.

Larry tapped a well-manicured finger against the armrest and straightened the razor-sharp pleat in his expensive dress slacks. His cold eyes regarded Greg thoughtfully. "There is a detective in the cubicle next to my brother's who told the police some absurd story about Paul trying to kill him the night before the wedding."

"What detective?"

"Eric something—"

"Henning?" Greg supplied.

"I don't know. They were moving him downstairs when I arrived. I never spoke to him, you understand. Wouldn't have paid any attention at all, but I heard him insisting he had to speak with McKella."

Greg found his dislike for this vain man growing in direct proportion to the man's lack of concern. "Why didn't you talk to him?"

Larry Patterson scowled. "I've been a bit busy, young man. It was my intention to look in on him this evening and find out what that drivel was all about."

"Where is he?" Greg demanded, standing up.

"They moved him to the third floor, I believe."

"Tell McKella to wait here. I'll be right back."

"Where are you going? Who do you think you are?"

Greg didn't bother to answer. A helpful nurse gave him Eric's room number.

Eric Henning proved to be a large, suspicious man, not at all dwarfed by the hospital equipment surrounding his powerful frame. He eyed Greg with open hostility, unwilling to part with any information until Greg explained the events that had taken place in Bermuda.

"Son of a bitch." Henning paused to cough. "I knew something was wrong as soon as my contact said he never heard of Dinsmore. If Dinsmore had really worked for Zuckerman's, this guy would have known him. I did some digging and stumbled over those ads his Lexington wife placed.''

Henning cocked an eyebrow. ''He was never divorced from her, you know. And Betty Jane wasn't the first one, either. There's a whole string of them. The bastard's a polygamist. Yet everyone who knew him claims he's the nicest damn guy.''

Including McKella. ''That's McConnel,'' Greg agreed bitterly.

Henning sat back wheezing for breath. ''Bastard punctured the lung,'' he explained, nodding toward his chest. He regarded Greg speculatively. ''What's your interest in all this?''

''I knew the real Paul Dinsmore.''

''Yeah?'' Henning looked skeptical.

''Yeah. He died in a car crash fifteen years ago.''

Henning nodded. ''You did your homework. I traced those records, too. Two cars, five young men.'' He paused to cough. ''Cops cited speed and alcohol. Everyone was pulled or thrown from the wrecks by the time the cops arrived. Three of the victims were still alive. Two teens from a local town and a hitchhiker the real Dinsmore picked up.''

The sights and sounds returned, as they frequently did in Greg's nightmares. A man screaming, writhing in the grass beside him, reeking of blood and gasoline and death. Greg shut his eyes against the memory, but that was never enough to stop the kaleidoscope of images.

Greg opened his eyes and found Henning watching steadily, judging him with piercing eyes.

''You got some sort of personal stake in all this?'' Henning's eyes bored into him. ''McKella's a real pretty lady.''

Greg stiffened at his tone. "Yes, she is."

Henning nodded as if he had just confirmed something. "Watch your back. If McConnel's the one who attacked me, he's quick with that knife. I never heard him coming until I felt the blade."

"You must have put up a fight."

Henning shook his head. "I shoulda, but all I did was claw him like a girl, trying to get that damn knife. I got in one blow to the chest, then he punctured the lung. Doctors tell me I was lucky I was rolling or his final thrust would have caught the heart."

A nurse bustled in to take his temperature and blood pressure.

Greg rose to leave, but the detective removed the thermometer from his mouth. "If you're going to take care of McKella, you'd better look into the process Kestler's working on. There's a lot of money involved."

"Mr. Henning, talk later." The nurse thrust the thermometer back in his mouth.

Henning promptly removed it again. "Find out what the old man was doing at the plant," he wheezed.

The nurse turned to Greg. "Sir, I'm going to have to ask you to step outside until I get these readings."

"I was just leaving."

"Tell McKella I'm sorry about her father," Henning mumbled around the thermometer. "Hope he pulls through okay."

"Sir!" The nurse scowled.

"And I'm gonna do some more checking as soon as I get out of here."

Greg knew a threat when he heard one. "Do that. I'll catch you later, Henning."

McKella met him at the elevator. "My uncle told me you were probably down here. Where's Eric?"

"Down the hall." He jerked his head to the right. "But you can't go in there right now. The nurse just threw me out." He took hold of her arm and turned her around, pressing the elevator button. "How's your dad?"

Her eyes brimmed with tears that she hastily blinked away. "He's holding his own, but his resistance is so weakened—I don't think he's going to make it, Greg."

"Hey, Pattersons aren't quitters, remember? Don't go counting him out yet."

She came into his arms with a small sound. Greg held her, stroking her hair and wishing he had more than banal words of comfort to offer. When she drew back, he wiped a teardrop from her cheek with the back of his knuckle. "Come on, it's late. I'll get you home."

"I need to run by the plant first."

Alarm snaked its way up his spine. "Why?"

"There was a fire in the lab. That's how they found my father."

"I know."

"But no one knows what Dad was doing there."

"McKella…"

"There are some things I need to check on, Greg." Determination lined her features.

"Do it tomorrow," he cajoled.

Amber eyes regarded him. "Why?"

"Because it's late. You're tired, your dad is ill—"

"Paul's still running around loose?" Her chin raised in a gesture he was coming to know only too well.

Greg groaned. She was too smart and too stubborn for her own good. "That, too."

"Paul couldn't have set that fire, Greg."

"I know. Let the police handle things, McKella."

"I will. I just need to check the accounts. Paul...I mean Jason...whoever he is—he has signature power."

His sense of alarm deepened. "Where's your uncle?"

"Upstairs with Dad."

"Shouldn't you stay here?"

"My father's unconscious, Greg. Only one more visitor can see him tonight and it's Uncle Larry's turn."

He knew her brave front was sheer bravado. She had to be running on pure nerves at this point. "We don't have a car, McKella. What do you suggest we do for transportation?"

"You don't have to come with me. This isn't your problem, Greg."

He didn't bother to respond, stepping aside to let her enter the elevator and depressing the button marked lobby. Her assumption that he would let her go alone irritated him. Didn't she understand they were in this together?

"Uncle Larry lent me his car keys. He'll catch a cab home," she said.

"Does he know where you're going?"

"Yes."

Greg tipped his head to study her. "He approved?"

"I've got his keys." She dangled them from her fingers.

Greg followed her outside, feeling edgy. Larry's car was a top of the line Mercedes-Benz with leather interior, gadgets galore and a built-in telephone. McKella headed for the driver's side, then stopped.

"Second thoughts?"

She cast him a dirty look. "Do you drive?"

"You want me to drive?"

"No, frankly, I want you to go back home, wherever that is, but somehow, I don't think you're going to do that at the moment."

"McKella…"

"Okay, darn it, the truth is, I can't see to drive."

He closed the gap between them in two long strides. "What is it? Let's get you back inside and have those x-rays—"

"No! It isn't that." She looked down to where his hands were gripping her forearms. "My contacts tore the morning of the wedding. There wasn't time to go home for a replacement set and my glasses were in my purse."

Greg's tension drained away, leaving a smile hovering at the corners of his mouth.

"If you laugh at me…"

"Wouldn't think of it."

"You are the most exasperating man."

"Thanks." He held out his hand for the keys. "But I'm a very good driver."

"You'd better be."

"Nice car," Greg offered as he slid behind the wheel.

"Do you think so? It's a little rich for my taste."

"Your uncle must make a good salary."

McKella shrugged. "Turn right at the next traffic light. Uncle Larry doesn't have anything else to spend his money on. His wife's been dead for years." She sent a puzzled glance his way. "Were you trying to imply something?"

"By saying it's a nice car?"

She made a face. "I get the feeling you don't like my uncle, Greg."

"Hey, I don't even know the man." He had to dodge

another car, which had come to a complete halt to make a right-hand turn.

McKella settled back against the seat. "My nerves are a bit raw at the moment," she told him.

"I noticed."

She flashed him a sad little smile. "Dad looked so old and shriveled somehow, lying there all hooked up like that. The odds aren't good, Greg. Not with the cancer eating him up inside." Her words trailed away. Greg reached down and placed a comforting hand on her thigh, wishing there was something he could say.

"Life isn't fair, 'Kella. But I'd never count Henry Patterson out."

Her smile was a little brighter as she directed him to turn off the main road. "You're right. We'll just have to wait and see what happens."

A tall gate blocked the entrance. Tucked some distance away behind the gate sat the sprawling brick building that housed Patterson Opticals.

"It doesn't look like anything is wrong from here."

Greg had to agree. The fire must have been contained quickly. He powered down the window and inserted the card McKella had pulled from the glove box. In ponderous slow motion, the gate swung open.

"Do you have live security?" he asked.

"A night watchman."

"Only one? No dogs?"

"One is enough. You need an identification card to go anywhere inside the building. We have a computer system that monitors everything."

Greg groaned. "You need a better security system. I could get inside this place in a heartbeat." A lone, battered pickup truck sat in the lot up front near the main entrance.

"You could not."

"Want me to prove it?"

"You'd set off alarms all over the place."

"Want to bet? This place is about as secure as a bus depot, McKella. Probably less so, because at least *there* you'd have a rent-a-cop or two."

"That isn't funny."

"It wasn't meant to be. Your outside fence is high, but it isn't electrified or wired. A person can go over it, under it or through it. Also, those cards are very fancy, but they don't work when the electricity goes out."

"We have a back-up system."

"Uh-huh. Computers are good tools. Great toys. Fun to operate. Easy to confuse."

"Excuse me. I thought you were an accountant, not a security expert."

Greg grinned. "One of the companies I saved was Azgaard Security."

He stopped the car, turned off the engine and twisted to face her.

"And I suppose another was a computer company?" she asked wryly.

He tapped her on the nose. "You're catching on. I can recommend Azgaard highly."

"No doubt you own a percentage of it?"

"No doubt."

"You're incorrigible."

"Yep. Want me to prove it?"

Something flickered across her expression, too quickly for him to decipher.

"I could break in and prove what I said," he offered.

"For now, let's just do it the easy way. It's late and

all I want is a quick glance around to assess the damage and pass the word that Paul isn't to be allowed inside.''

"The fire department will have roped the area off," he warned.

"Uncle Larry says I can still see inside."

"Uh-huh."

"Greg, you're seeing bogeymen behind every bush."

"Well, maybe you'd better start watching the bushes."

"What's that supposed to mean?"

"Someone tried to shove you down a flight of stairs today. Have you forgotten?" Anger at her close escape lent a curt tone to his words.

She shuddered. "Hardly. I'm so stiff I can barely move."

He sighed and rubbed her thigh gently. Her gaze flew from his hand to his face. He liked the way she became disconcerted whenever she started thinking of him in a sexual way.

Immediately, her business persona resurfaced. "I won't be long. You can wait out here—"

"Alone in the dark? I don't think so." He stroked the material covering her leg. A pulse point jumped to life in her neck. His fingers moved up to caress the side of her face, and he marveled anew at the softness of her skin.

"You're a big boy, Greg," she said breathlessly.

"Glad you noticed." He smiled when she blushed. "Are you sure you're okay?" he asked before she could chastise him.

Her amber eyes were wide and watchful. "Yes. I...I'm fine. Just a little stiff."

A fine tremor shivered through his body. She was so

unbelievably sweet. He tried to remind himself that he was the wrong man for this woman.

"It's nice of you to worry…" she began hesitantly.

He shook his head. "I'm not a nice man, remember?"

His fingers stopped their stroking to cup her cheek. She stared at him, barely breathing, and he gave in to the irresistible temptation to close the distance between them.

"Gre—"

His lips captured the sound of his name. McKella tensed for just a second, then her hands slid to his shoulders—to pull him closer, not to push him away.

Satisfied, he allowed his tongue to explore her mouth. She made a tiny sound of contentment that sent ripples of need along his hardening body. He slid his arm around her, drawing her closer…and his elbow jabbed the horn.

Chapter Eight

They broke apart like startled children. He could taste her sweetness in his mouth, and he wanted more. She pressed two shaky fingers against her trembling lips and Greg fought a powerful need to draw her back against him, to taste her more deeply.

"That shouldn't have happened."

Her words were soft whips, reminding him of all the reasons he couldn't claim this woman. Not now, not ever.

"If you expect me to apologize..."

A quick shake of her head. "I don't." Her hand reached for the door handle and she was out of the car before he could stop her. "Coming?"

"Damn." He took his time stepping from the car, surveying the dark parking lot. "Whose truck?" he asked to give himself time to recover from the devastating effect she had on his senses.

"That belongs to Ralph, the watchman."

"It's too dark out here." He came around the car and joined her on the sidewalk. She wouldn't meet his eyes.

"We turn out the lights late at night to save money."

"Believe me, the amount you're saving isn't worth

the risk of this dark lot. Let's go inside and get this over with.''

''I told you it's not necessary for you to come with me. In fact—''

He stopped her words with a shake of his head. ''Sorry. I just don't like this situation. Too many things are happening around you. I'm worried, okay?'' He reached for her arm, wishing he had the right to touch her in other ways, but knowing he didn't dare.

''Okay.''

He turned away from her vulnerable expression before he could give in to the savage impulses yammering inside him. ''You want to go look at the damage, we'll go look at the damage.''

Inside, a portly man whose belt supported his stomach hurried forward to open the second set of double glass doors. From behind the reception desk came the unmistakable sound of a television. Two soft drink cans, a bag of potato chips and a half-eaten candy bar littered the otherwise pristine surface of the rounded desk.

''Ms. Patterson…I mean, Mrs. Dinsmore…I wasn't expecting you. How's your father doing?''

''Holding his own, Ralph. Were you the one who found him?''

''No, ma'am. That would be the fire department. They made a quick check of the building.''

''Looking for my father?''

''No, ma'am. Just as a precaution. We didn't know anyone was in the building.''

''My father didn't sign in?''

Ralph scratched his balding head, distress pleating his features. ''Well, no. Now that you come to mention it…''

McKella flashed Greg a dark look. Wisely, he said nothing. "Mr. Wyman and I will be taking a look around, Ralph."

"Sure. You want me to go with you? The fire didn't spread past the lab, but the smoke carried through the ventilation system. They had to close everything down."

"The lab doesn't have its own system?" Greg asked.

"No," McKella answered. "It's supposed to self-seal in the event of a fire or an alarm being tripped. Want to say 'I told you so,' now?"

"Think I'll pass. Thanks just the same."

"Uh, you both should sign in, Ms.—Mrs. Dinsmore."

"Of course."

Ralph hurried back to the desk. "I've got a flashlight right here. Power's off in the lab. I'm not even supposed to go inside, just take a quick look around is all, but I don't guess it matters if *you* do. Go inside, I mean."

McKella gave Greg an I-dare-you-to-say-a-word look. He grinned at her, knowing words from him would be superfluous at this point.

He followed her through the labyrinth of corridors. While there was light, he allowed himself to enjoy the subtle sway of her hips. The material of the sexy blue jumpsuit whispered provocatively over her body.

"Before you leave, let me have the phone number for that security firm you recommended," she tossed over her shoulder.

"You got it." He was amazed when his voice came out sounding relatively normal, and thankful when they reached the area where the lights disappeared and

McKella had to turn on the flashlight. Unfortunately, he couldn't turn off his randy thoughts quite so easily.

Smoke clung to the air, the smell growing stronger the closer they got. The police department's yellow tape roped off the lab. Without the flashlight, they wouldn't have been able to see a thing. The scene was eerie enough for a horror movie. Greg's earlier apprehension returned with a vengeance.

"Poor Ben," McKella murmured. She aimed the flashlight for the darkest, most scorched area. "That was his research area. I'm glad we keep back-up files upstairs as well as in the vault. I just hope his were up to date."

His sense of alarm increased the longer they stood there, easy targets in the darkness with their telltale flashlight beam. "You have a vault in here?"

McKella swung the light toward a dark metal door not far from the worst of the fire damage. "Over there. It was here when Dad bought the place."

"Maybe we'd better go upstairs and have a look at those back-up files, McKella."

"Yes. I think we'd better," she agreed with slow deliberation.

"Any idea why your father would have been in the building last night?"

She raised her head to look at him. "Only the same idea you have. Dad must have discovered something about Paul—Jason."

"Stick with Paul," he told her, watching the darkness. "As far as the police know, you don't know him by any other name. And this doesn't have to be about your husband, McKella. Maybe your father came to see your uncle."

Hair slapped her cheek as she shook her head. "Dad

is pretty much bedridden. Only something extreme would have dragged him down here.''

He resisted an impulse to touch her—definitely not a good idea. ''McKella, there's something I think you'd better know. Four years ago, when I did that audit, there was money missing.''

She jerked her head in astonished disbelief. ''What are you talking about?''

''Your father paid back what your uncle owed and I straightened out the books afterwards.''

''Are you saying my uncle stole from Patterson?''

He hadn't wanted to be the one to tell her. ''Your father called it 'borrowing.' He said your uncle had several investments turn bad on him all at once and he used company funds to bail himself out.''

''I don't believe this.''

Greg sighed. ''I wouldn't have mentioned it, but I think we should take a quick look at the books while we're here.'' Even in the reflected light from the flashlight, he could see her shock.

''You're saying my uncle is a crook?''

''No. I'm saying he borrowed some money once. Your dad must not think he was a crook or he wouldn't have let him continue running the accounting department.'' Greg didn't add that people had blind spots and, apparently, Larry was one of her father's. ''I just thought you should know.''

McKella faced him in the eerie light cast by the flashlight. ''Why?''

''This process Kestler's working on is going to be worth a lot of money, am I right? Did you ever hear of industrial spying?''

''Now you think my uncle is a spy?''

''Don't jump to conclusions. But Henning suggested

we take a close look at Kestler's process. That's where the big money is and people generally commit crimes for gain.''

McKella resumed walking until they reached a section of hallway that was dimly lit. She snapped off the flashlight. ''What else did you and Eric talk about?''

''He thinks your husband was the one who stabbed him the night before your wedding.''

A bleak look crossed her face, but she straightened her shoulders and headed for a stairwell. Without a word, she led the way to the executive offices upstairs. The smell of smoke lingered even here.

They entered what had been her father's modest office four years ago. McKella flicked on the wall switch and let out a startled gasp. The safe hung open, as did a file drawer and one of the desk drawers. Someone had rifled the office—in a big hurry.

''Who had the combination to the safe?'' Greg asked.

''Paul, Dad, Uncle Larry, me and Denise, Dad's secretary of twenty years.''

''Was your husband using this office?''

''Yes.'' She headed for the safe and peered inside without touching anything.

''Can you tell what's missing?''

''Maybe. Eventually.''

''Your books?''

''Computerized.''

''I know. The back-up disks and hard copies?''

''Don't you know where they are?''

''I know where they *were*.''

''Well, they're still kept in the same place—my uncle's wall safe.''

He followed her to the accounting department. Her

uncle's safe also stood open—the only thing that had been touched in the more opulently appointed room.

"They aren't here," McKella told him.

"I didn't think they would be."

"You think my uncle did this?" she challenged.

"Or your husband, hoping to make your uncle look guilty. The other back-up material is in the vault?"

"Yes, but we can't get in without electricity."

"There must be a fail-safe."

"Probably, but I don't know what it is."

He shook his head. "I thought you owned this company."

McKella spun and headed back the way they had come.

"Where are you going?" he asked.

"To look at the vault."

"McKella, we should get out of here and phone the police." The alarm he'd been feeling had become clanging sirens in his head. He wanted her away from here. Now.

"A quick look, then we'll call." She headed through the door at the end of the hall, bypassing the elevator as she started down the steps. "What's wrong with you?"

Hell, there were a number of ways to answer that, he thought without humor, but he could see there was no stopping her. "What if whoever did this is still inside the building?"

"Then it can't be my uncle, can it? We just left him at the hospital."

"McKella—"

"Why would Paul stick around? He's already got what he came for." She entered the corridor. "We'll just take a quick look, I promise." She reached the lab, ducked under the police tape and entered the crime scene.

"What else do you keep in the vault?"

"Chemicals. Experiments. I don't really know. It isn't all that big."

"Would a person fit inside?"

"Sure. There's room for two or three people. Why?"

"Just a thought." A nasty one. No point in adding to her worries, but he couldn't help thinking that a vault was a great place for a person to hide. "Who has access?"

"Just the people who work here. Six—no, seven, total."

McKella came to a halt with a muttered imprecation. Greg didn't have to ask why. In the beam of her light, they could clearly see the vault standing open before them.

"Greg, it was closed earlier," she whispered.

Hairs lifted on the back of his scalp as she started forward. "McKella, don't go in there."

As he reached to push her aside, someone lunged at them from the inky blackness. The flashlight flew from McKella's hand, crashing to the floor, plunging the room into complete darkness.

Hard fingers grasped his arm like a vise. Greg wrenched himself backward in an effort to break that bruising hold. He heard the pop as sudden pain swamped him, and his left arm suddenly dangled, useless. A blow landed across his back, catching his damaged shoulder. He collapsed to his knees, scraping his leg. Trying to block the pain, his right hand searched for something to use as a weapon.

There was the sound of another scuffle. McKella!

A flash of orange flame licked the darkness in a deafening roar of sound. Greg tried to get to his feet. McKella cried out and then the sounds abruptly stilled.

"Stay where you are or I'll kill her," a voice announced.

Greg froze in recognition. Where had the bastard gotten a gun? "Kill us, and who will you blame this time, Jason?" He baited the man in an effort to draw attention away from McKella. He couldn't see a thing.

"Shut up!" Jason yelled.

But if Greg couldn't see, then neither could his opponent. Another commotion began. Greg surged to his feet.

"Ow," Jason yelled. McKella was fighting back.

The sound of a slap sent Greg lunging forward. The second gunshot seemed to reverberate in his head. He crashed into the two struggling bodies and his weak leg buckled without warning. He heard the gun clatter to the floor as his bad shoulder struck the frame of the heavy vault door. Waves of pain rolled over him.

McKella yelped. Greg tried to rise—and failed. She stumbled over him and went sprawling face down. He scrambled toward her, pain screaming through his body as he bumped against a shelf.

They were inside the vault.

He twisted around as the heavy door slammed shut against his shoulder. The pain was so intense, he closed his eyes, unable to move.

"Greg! Don't you dare be dead!" McKella rushed to his side. Her arms tugged at him, adding to his pain.

Greg moaned. "Not dead," he managed past gritted teeth. She'd lifted him so that he was half sitting, half lying, his head nestled against the softness of her breasts.

"Any...other time...I'd enjoy this," he panted past the hurt. "You okay?"

A tear splashed against his cheek. McKella was crying. McKella never cried. She was strong. He'd kill her husband with his bare hands.

"You fool," she sobbed brokenly. "You had to go and be a hero. Where did he shoot you?"

Greg tried to shake his head and found he couldn't. Her hands pinned him in place, but pain kept him from appreciating the position.

"Need...your help," he got out.

"Tell me what to do."

"Shoulder."

"He shot you in the shoulder?"

"No...dislocated again, damn it." He sucked air past his gritted teeth. "You've got...to put it back."

She pulled away, inadvertently jerking his entire body. "Are you crazy? I'm not a doctor. I barely passed CPR training."

Greg used his right arm to lever himself all the way into a sitting position. The movement was sheer torture. "Heart's fine," he pushed out, "but...if you don't want me to pass out..." Greg battled the rising nausea.

McKella reached for him. Her fingers traced a path down the side of his face and neck. They skimmed across his shoulder and stilled when they reached the socket. "Oh, my God, Greg."

"Just...push it...back in place."

"I can't!" But her fingers continued to explore the injury with delicate care, tracing the joint and the damage.

He leaned his head against the metal door, thankful for the cool sensation as he summoned the effort to insist that she had no choice. Still protesting, McKella shifted positions and bumped his bad leg, once more jarring his body.

Greg groaned and sank into a well of pain.

"GREG! OH DAMN." McKella bit down on her lip, tasting blood. She'd barely touched him. Dear God, how was she supposed to pull his shoulder back into its socket? She'd never be able to do this.

He uttered a sound of distress.

"Greg! Wake up. You have to tell me what to do."

"Not…sleeping. Get…behind."

She scooted around behind him, careful this time not to bump his body.

"Have to…feel your way. Pull down…then back up. Nurse…leaned me over a gurney…last time."

"We don't have a gurney!"

Greg didn't respond.

"Greg?"

All she could hear was the labored sound of his breathing. Had he passed out? Oh, God.

Crying, cursing, she propped the back of his head against her chest. A shelving unit dug into her back, but she welcomed the leverage.

Taking his injured shoulder in both hands, she inhaled deeply. Before she could change her mind, she forced the joint out and down, then back up, with a strength she hadn't known she possessed. She cursed as he cried out, terrified that she was doing him irreparable harm. With a sudden *snap* the injured socket reconnected. Greg slumped against her chest, unmoving. McKella leaned her head back against the metal shelf and sobbed.

"McKella," he whispered hoarsely after a while, "it's all right. You did good."

Though she heard his quiet words, she couldn't stem the flow of tears. She cried for Greg, for her father, for the faces of the two dead women who would haunt her nightmares. She cried for herself and her gullibility—and her sense of utter helplessness.

Greg shifted and groaned. "McKella, sweetheart, you've got to stop crying. We need to get out of here."

She wasn't sure that she could take any more. This nightmare just went on and on. Wiping at the stream of tears with the back of one hand, her other hand traced the path of his shoulder.

"My shoulder's fine, McKella, but I banged up my bad leg when I fell. I think it's bleeding. Where'd he get a gun anyhow?"

"Uncle Larry had one in his safe." Unable to see anything in the encompassing darkness, McKella felt her way down his body to check his leg.

"I wish you'd do that sometime when we're not in the middle of a crisis," he rasped in an obvious effort to tease her.

McKella hiccuped a laugh despite her tears. "Wait here," she directed.

"What's my other option?"

McKella swept the concrete floor with her hands, moving away from him to widen the search.

"What are you doing?" he asked.

"Looking for the flashlight."

"Are you sure it's in here?"

"No." Her fingers found something, but it wasn't a flashlight. She released the object and continued, moving slowly, carefully.

"You sure do know how to reassure a man."

"Being reassuring is your job. I'm supposed to be the helpless woman here."

"Ha! A mama bear should be so helpless."

She tried to match his banter, because talking held her terror at bay. "Are you commenting on my grouchiness now, Wyman?"

She heard him shift position, heard another indrawn hiss of air and prayed he wasn't seriously hurt. She continued to sweep layers of dust from the floor with her bare hands.

"Wouldn't think of it," he told her. "And if I did, I sure as heck wouldn't say so out loud."

"Smart man." Her fingers closed over the rubber haft of the flashlight. "Got it!" She fumbled for the switch. Nothing happened. "Work, you worthless piece of junk." She cursed again and gave the object a harsh shake, knocking it against the floor. A beam of light flickered, then held steady, illuminating their tiny prison.

"Impressive," Greg told her. "Whenever *I* curse like that, I fear lightning bolts. *You* get light."

McKella swung the beam toward his face, and he shut his eyes. She immediately lowered the light, but not before seeing how pale and drawn his features were. She ran the beam down his body to his thigh. Blood soaked his jeans around a jagged tear that went straight across the outside edge.

"You cut yourself," she told him.

"Yeah. It hurts."

She tried for a light tone to cover her fear. "Don't be a baby."

"I'm a man, it's my God-given right."

McKella laughed out loud. Greg was incorrigible *and* outrageous, but he did know how to take the tension out of the situation.

"It had to be my *bad* leg," Greg muttered.

"Well, you wouldn't want two bad legs now, would you?"

"Good point. I'll try to remember that in my agony."

McKella chuckled again as she knew he'd meant her to do. She stood and looked at the door. "If you can move over a bit, I'll get us out of here."

"Nice trick if you can do it."

"The vault only locks from the outside," she assured him. "The purpose is to keep strangers out, not employees in."

Greg shifted as she stepped around his injured leg and pulled the handle. Nothing happened. She yanked down once more, putting weight behind her movement. Still nothing.

"Problem?"

"It isn't opening."

"I can see that. Let me try."

"Don't stand up, you'll do more damage to..."

Greg used his good hand on the shelving unit to climb to his feet, but the effort that action took was reflected in the sound of his harsh breathing. He applied his good shoulder against the door. The metal didn't budge even when McKella added her weight.

"Heat from the fire may have jammed something," he suggested. "Or else Jason set something heavy against the outside. Either way, I don't think we're going anywhere real soon."

Greg turned his back to the door and slid back down. "I don't suppose we have a roll of gauze and some tape in here anywhere?"

McKella directed the flashlight to the orderly shelves. "We've got packing tape. No gauze. If I had some scissors I could cut off the bottom of my jumpsuit.''

"That sounds promising. I'll help."

"You would." She sat down next to him. "Don't worry. Ralph will come looking for us soon."

"You're making the assumption that he's in a condition to come looking," he muttered.

The veiled suggestion that Paul might have harmed the friendly guard brought McKella's feeling of horror rushing back.

"Hey, you okay?" Greg asked.

She focused on his face. "Peachy. How about you?"

"My head hurts, my back hurts, my shoulder hurts and my leg alternates between burning pain and cramped aching. I'd say I'm doing pretty good."

"You're hopeless." McKella rose, flashlight in hand.

"Hey, where are you going?"

"To check the files we came in here for."

"They won't be there."

Greg was right. The printed files were gone, as was the sample tray. "He's going to sell Ben's process, isn't he?"

"He's going to try."

"I wish I had kicked him harder and higher."

"Me, too. Pull up some concrete."

McKella frowned. "How come you aren't worried?"

"Don't kid yourself. I'm plenty worried, but there isn't a thing we can do right now." His voice betrayed his strain. "Besides, here we are, all alone. I could have my wicked way with you."

She plunked down beside him. "I detect a serious lack of menace here."

"Hey," he protested.

"One wrong move and I only need to aim for your leg or your shoulder for all your brave talk to be history."

Greg heaved a theatrical sigh and winced in earnest. "I hate an intelligent woman."

"Not so intelligent," she argued morosely. "I married Paul."

He reached for her hand. "But you saw through him. You never loved him."

"I never loved him, but I didn't see through him, Greg. I didn't believe a word you said at first."

"Seducing women is what he does for a living, McKella."

Small comfort for her wounded pride. "If he seduced women for a living, then how come he couldn't bear to—?" She bit back the words, but not soon enough.

"Couldn't bear to what?"

"Nothing."

"He couldn't seduce you?"

McKella squirmed, searching for a topic to divert him. His fingers trailed up her arm, sending currents tingling through her.

"Don't be embarrassed, McKella," he said softly. "That just proves my point. He knew you could see through his act every time he touched you."

Greg reached across her body, making her jump. She caught his knowing expression before he clicked off the flashlight. "Let's save the batteries in case we need them later."

"Greg—"

"Besides, it's cozier this way. Reminds me of Bermuda—before the storm hit."

The last thing she wanted to be reminded of was Bermuda. And she was already too aware of him for any degree of comfort. She wiggled a bit and he slid his good arm around her, pulling her closer.

"Greg—"

His hand stroked her arm.

"Greg, this isn't wise," she felt compelled to point out, but she didn't move away from his soothing touch.

"I'm in no condition to do more than talk at the moment."

"Good. Then you can answer questions. I have a million of them."

"I have a better idea."

His hand moved to the nape of her neck, fingers sliding through her hair until he cupped the back of her head. The sensuality behind his action shocked her, even as his other hand held her face. In the utter darkness of the vault, she was unable to see his shape, let alone his expression, but she could feel the crisp whorls of hair on his hard chest.

"We'll get to your questions…later," he promised. The low timbre of his voice threaded the darkness, entwining them in intimacy. "I need to run an experiment, first." Gently, he pulled her head towards him.

"But—"

"Hush." His breath whispered across her cheek, brushing her skin, somehow circumventing her internal alarms. McKella shivered, pulling his head to hers.

"Your skin is so soft, 'Kella," he murmured against her lips. "Soft—" he nipped the lower lip ever so lightly with his teeth "—sweet" he licked the spot he had just nipped "—tantalizing." And then his lips were there, demanding a response that she found herself anxious to give.

His tongue invaded her mouth, stroking her to incredible passion. She moaned, undulating in an effort to get closer to the source of such pleasure. Her hands roamed his back, her straining nipples pressing against the thin materials that separated her from the hard wall of his chest.

So this was how it should be.

"What are you doing to me?" she whispered when his lips drew back.

Greg made a sound like a strangled chuckle. "If you don't know, then he was a worse lover than I thought."

Like ice water, the words doused her, shaking her from her sensual haze. "This can't be happening."

"It's not anymore," he said in resignation.

"That isn't funny. Why did you kiss me?"

"I had the impression the kiss was a mutual undertaking."

"No. I mean, it was, but it shouldn't have been. I'm still married."

"To the wrong man."

His low voice was coated by rough edges, but it was his next words that sent tremors through her nerves.

"You can't keep throwing that marriage in my face forever. When this is over, McKella, when your husband is no longer a barrier, we'll finish what we just started."

"I barely know you." She cursed her voice for giving away her uncertainty.

"You know me," he said quietly. "I'm the man who's falling in love with you."

Her stifled gasp hung in the silence. Emotions flowed through her, too quick to catalog. "You can't love me."

"I agree. It defies common sense. I should be run-

ning for safety. I plan to die a bachelor, you know.''
The quaver in his voice belied the teasing tone.

"Don't worry," she assured him. "Your bachelor-
hood is safe from me, no matter what happens. Once
I'm free of Paul, I intend to remain free. I wouldn't
marry again at gunpoint.''

"Fine, no shotguns.''

"I'm serious, Greg.''

He sighed. "Okay, we'll just live together...until the
children come.''

Images clashed with her resolve. She had wanted a
child so badly. But having Greg's baby was...
unthinkable. This hollow yearning sensation must be
born of fear, not desire.

"I suppose you want to start your own dynasty,''
she said sharply.

Greg shifted, brushing his bad leg against hers in an
effort to straighten it again. "A dynasty, huh? Nope.
The world already has a lot of people. But I think three
is a manageable number. Small enough to give plenty
of attention to each child, but large enough to make a
well-rounded family unit.''

Words jammed her throat like the emotions jamming
her brain. She fought back tears that sprang from nowhere. He was calmly discussing her dreams in his
whiskey-soft voice, and she thought her heart would
break with the pain.

Without warning, the vault door clicked noisily.
They barely moved away before the heavy metal
swung outward. The bright beam of a flashlight trapped
them in its blinding glare.

Chapter Nine

Greg was heartily sick of questions, nurses, doctors, and hospitals in that order. And if one more cop asked him one more question...

"Ah, Mr. Wyman. Here you are."

Arrested in his feeble attempt to sit up using only his unstrapped arm for support, Greg stared at the lanky dark-skinned detective standing next to his curtained cubicle.

"Freer? I don't believe it. A little out of your jurisdiction, aren't you?"

Freer displayed his perfect white teeth in a wide smile. "I am relieved to see you do not discriminate, Mr. Wyman. You give your local constables a disagreeable workload as well as we poor island men."

"What are you doing here?"

The detective arched an expressive eyebrow.

"Am I under arrest?" Greg demanded.

"Now why would you make that assumption, Mr. Wyman?" He reached forward and helped Greg sit up with firm but gentle strength.

"Call it paranoia, but I don't think you left your comfortable island and flew over here on a social call. We've only been gone a few hours."

Freer smiled again. "Indeed, and yet here you are. Another country, another hospital, another situation. Ironic, would you not say?"

"Painful," Greg corrected. "I'd call it painful. Would you hand me what's left of my pants?"

"Oh, good, you found him," McKella announced. Her voice preceded her into the narrow cubicle. Her hair was tousled, her face smudged with dirt, and there was a new bruise forming on her forehead. Greg thought she looked wonderful.

She tipped her head to one side and studied him. "You look terrible," she told him.

There was no doubting the twinkle in Freer's eyes this time as the men exchanged looks.

"Her sweet talk goes straight to my head," Greg explained.

"They want you to spend the night," McKella informed Greg briskly.

"I already told them to forget it. Besides, it's nearly morning."

"Greg, you need to rest. They took five stitches—"

"Seven," he corrected. "Trust me, I counted each one. The numbing agent didn't kick in until after they finished, and the shot hurt worse than the needle they sewed me with."

"Why are men always such babies?" she asked Freer.

"Hey!" Greg protested.

She braced her hands on her hips and glared at him. "At least a woman wouldn't take out her frustration on the poor nurse."

"That 'poor nurse' outweighs me by twenty pounds and has the same tender touch as a drill press."

"See what I mean?" she beseeched Freer. "You'll

never get any cooperation out of him when he's like this.''

Greg turned his attention to the detective who was, as usual, quietly watching both of them. "What am I supposed to cooperate with? What *are* you doing here?"

"I have questions," Freer told him mildly.

"Trunk lines down again?" Greg asked.

The detective raised and lowered his shoulders a scant inch in his equivalent of a shrug. The man had made understatement an art form.

"I always intended to visit this part of your country. When the opportunity presented itself, I seized the occasion."

"What opportunity?" But the nurse chose that moment to squeeze her substantial form in beside the other two.

"If you're really determined to abdicate our sanctuary," she told Greg in a nasal whine laced with sarcasm, "you need to sign this release form."

"'Abdicate our sanctuary?'" Greg repeated.

The nurse sniffed and handed him a clipboard and a sheaf of papers. "These are the instructions for dealing with the sutures and your shoulder. This is a prescription for pain which, given what a macho type you are, you probably will discard." She glared at him down her long nose. "And this needs to be signed here and here. You'll need to see your own doctor next week to have the stitches removed."

Greg accepted the clipboard and the pen and signed as she indicated. "I think I'll just gnaw them out with my teeth instead," he told her.

The nurse sniffed again. "Suit yourself. The mouth

is a haven for germs you know, but I just love a tough guy.''

Greg chuckled out loud as she took back the clipboard and turned to give the other two a victorious smile. ''Take him with my blessing.'' And she disappeared back through the curtain.

''You do have a way with women,'' McKella told him. ''Need some help getting dressed?''

Chafing under her glare, he shook his head—and immediately wished he hadn't. ''We macho types are tough. I'll just go home naked.''

''Here, I got you some clothing. The other stuff is a mess.''

''Thanks.'' He lifted the green surgical scrubs.

McKella made a face. ''Don't ask. Just put them on over your other pants. Trust me, you'll get fewer looks in those than in your own clothing.''

''I fear my counterpart and I need to ask you a few questions before you leave,'' Freer interrupted.

''Counterpart?''

''Officer Stone,'' McKella explained. ''He's the investigating officer on the lab fire. He's talking with the doctor right now.''

''No, actually, I'm right here.''

Greg studied the newcomer and recognized a career cop in the hard lines of his cynical face.

''Wyman? Your doctor says you're free to go.''

''I'm trying, God knows, I'm trying.''

''First, mind telling me what you were doing on the other side of the police tape?''

''I told you—'' McKella began. The officer held up a broad hand.

''Mrs. Dinsmore, would you mind waiting in the

hall? I'd like to hear Mr. Wyman's answers to the questions.''

''But—''

''McKella, see if you can keep Nurse Harridan out of here until I get dressed,'' Greg asked.

For a long moment, he held her gaze. Irritation, anger and a trace of fear tumbled behind her amber eyes. She cared. She might not *want* to, but she cared. Greg smiled. Irritation won out in her expression.

''No problem. Is there anything else you'd like? Some coffee? Your slippers?'' She turned and whirled through the curtain.

Greg looked at the men looming over his bed and grimaced. ''She's had a long couple of days.''

''Indeed,'' Freer agreed.

''About what happened,'' Stone prodded.

Greg nodded and reached for the pants. He related the events and answered questions, wondering all the while if the police had finally penetrated his own deception.

Eventually, Stone was called away. Greg regarded Freer. ''I'd still like to know what brought you here. I'm surprised you'd come stateside just to ask a few questions.''

''A private plane left the island shortly before the hurricane restricted air traffic yesterday. The plane was registered here in Kentucky, Mr. Wyman.''

Greg shook his head. ''I don't understand.''

''The aircraft was registered to Franklin Harvey of Louisville, Kentucky.''

''Should I know him?''

''Mr. Harvey is currently in Paris, France, touring with his wife and family. No one had permission or authorization to use his plane, let alone his name.''

"What does that have to do with me or McKella?"

Freer cocked an eyebrow. "Perhaps nothing. Do you believe in coincidence, Mr. Wyman?"

Greg felt grim. "No."

"Precisely. Do you know anyone connected with this case who is a pilot?"

Greg shook his head. "But didn't the pilot have to clear customs?"

"Indeed. It appears phoney documents were used. Your local police department tells me they are not that difficult to obtain. Any thoughts on this, Mr. Wyman?"

Greg reached for the shirt and realized he would be unable to get it on with his arm taped to his shoulder. "Anyone can hire a pilot. Hell, if they know where to look, anyone can hire a killer."

Freer leaned over and helped him into the shirt, pulling it over the sling housing his left arm. "Go on."

"The only one who benefits from the murder of Betty Jane is McKella's husband. He'd also benefit from the death of Eleanor Beauchamp in that there'd be one less person to testify against him. You're no fool, Constable. Even you can see he wanted McKella's company. Failing that, he went after the process this Kestler guy is developing. There's big money in corporate espionage these days."

"And the incident with McKella in the stairwell?"

Greg rubbed his jaw. "Had to be her husband."

"Why?"

"Maybe he still thought he could inherit the company."

Freer's expression said he'd expected better. Greg shrugged, then wished he hadn't.

"Have you spoken with McKella's detective yet?"

Freer nodded. "Mr. Henning was most helpful."

"Then you know her marriage is a sham."

"That is what Mr. Henning tells us."

"Find her husband," Greg demanded. "She won't be safe until you do."

"We will, Mr. Wyman. We will."

He helped Greg stand, and they pushed through the curtain to find McKella waiting by the nurse's station. Greg liked the way her eyes lit when she saw him. She walked to his side, her concern for him clear.

"Are you okay?"

"Fine," he told her, laying his hand on her shoulder.

Officer Stone moved down the hospital corridor, a new crease on his lined face. "Freer? I've got another call. Come on. I need to roll."

McKella and Greg promised to hold themselves available for more questions, then watched the two men leave through the emergency room doors.

"I don't think I'd like being a policeman," McKella said thoughtfully.

"Permanent heartburn," he agreed. He slanted her a speculative look. "So where should we spend the night?"

She smiled, a look that said she was finally in control of something. "Given your chivalrous nature, and to forestall a situation like the one we found ourselves in at the hotel in Bermuda, I've booked us into a local hotel tonight."

"You have?"

She appeared gratified by his surprise. "Yes."

Glumly, he regarded her. "Separate rooms, I suppose?"

"Of course."

"I was afraid you were going to say that."

"You're all talk, Wyman."

Greg wiggled his eyebrows. "Want to share a room again and prove that?"

"No." She hesitated. "Would you mind if I ran upstairs for a few minutes before we leave? It can wait if you're hurting or—"

His gaze softened in understanding. "I'll go with you."

"I know they won't let me in since it's long past visiting hours, but I just wanted to check with the nurse—"

"Good idea. Come on."

The night nurse proved to be a sympathetic young woman. Since all the patients except Henry Patterson had been moved out of the ICU, she agreed to allow McKella to see her father for a few minutes.

Greg smiled and kissed her on the forehead before folding himself into a chair in the waiting room. "Take your time. I'll wait," he promised.

Her father lay as she had seen him last, the hum and blip of the monitors his only companions. Tears misted her eyes as she stared at the tubes attached to his once-strong body.

"I love you, Dad."

She lifted a veined hand and stroked the back of it with her fingers. "There's so much I need to talk to you about." Sitting next to his bed, she began to recite the events of the past few days.

"To make matters worse, I think I'm falling in love with Greg." She stopped in dismay, shocked by the revelation. The truth was frightening, particularly when she realized that she had just paraphrased Greg's words to her. *I'm the man who's falling in love with you.*

"It must be the stress," she hurried to explain. "I barely know him. I can't be in love. I'm not even sure

I'd recognize love if it came up and bit me.'' She stroked her father's sunken cheek, thinking his face had more color now than when she'd first entered the room.

"Besides, I think Greg may be Paul's baby brother.''

The idea of the men being related left an unpalatable taste in her mouth.

"There's a resemblance between them, but their animosity is frightening. Brothers shouldn't hate each other like that. On the other hand, Greg thinks Paul killed their father.'' She paused, fighting an urge to cry.

Did her father's eyelids flicker the least little bit? McKella stared at his face for several seconds. This time she was almost certain she saw a flicker of movement behind his closed eyes. Dare she hope he was reacting to her words? Or at least to the sound of her voice? McKella pushed forward with her one-way conversation.

"Paul may have killed Betty Jane, but he has nothing to gain by my death," she reminded her father as well as herself. "Uncle Larry does, but can you see him killing me to gain control of the company?''

The machines blipped in mocking answer.

"Ms. Patterson?''

The nurse stood in the doorway. "We have a patient arriving in a few minutes so I'll have to ask you to leave. You should go home and get some rest. If anything changes, we'll call you.''

Too weary to argue, McKella placed a kiss on her father's cheek and gave his hand another gentle squeeze.

She found Greg asleep in a chair in the waiting room. His face was tipped to one side, looking almost relaxed despite the bruises and faint signs of strain.

McKella pushed back the curl of hair that had fallen

across his forehead and found herself abruptly staring into cloudy blue-green eyes.

"Let's get you into a more comfortable bed," she whispered.

"There's an offer I won't refuse." His voice was husky with sleep, but his eyes cleared quickly and focused. They were level with her chest.

McKella drew back, tingling where his eyes had seemed to touch her. "You have a one-track mind."

"What did I say?" he protested, but he gave her a lopsided grin as he rose painfully. "How's your dad?"

It would be so easy to love this man.

They talked quietly as they waited for a cab and rode along the silent streets. Her uncle's car was still in the lot at Patterson's, since she'd ridden to the hospital in the ambulance with Greg. She'd have to make arrangements to get it later.

The hotel clerk regarded their attire suspiciously, but McKella wasn't in the mood for nonsense. She used her most official tone of voice and declined the use of a bellhop since their luggage was still in her uncle's car out at the plant. The clerk frowned, watching as they crossed to the elevator. No doubt he'd send hotel security to check on them, but at least they rode the elevator to the fourth floor alone.

"Nicely done," Greg told her as he leaned against the back wall.

"Are you okay?" She shook her head. "Stupid question. Of course you aren't. You look exhausted."

"Yeah. At the moment, I'm not real sure I can even get out of this elevator."

The doors slid open, and she reached for his waist. "Lean on me. You should have stayed in the hospital."

"Probably."

He swayed slightly while she fumbled to open the door with his card key. "We have adjoining rooms," she told him.

"Good."

"Do you need some help, Greg?" His look of depletion reminded her of the night of the storm.

"No, thanks. I'm just going to fall into bed. I'll leave the connecting door unlocked."

McKella wondered at her feeling of disappointment. Why was she feeling rejected? Had she expected a repeat of their night after the storm?

"Get some sleep," she chided softly.

"I'm halfway there."

She didn't want to leave him, she realized. What if he needed something in the night?

"I'm going to open the connecting doors so you can call me if you need anything." She stood on tiptoe to place a gentle kiss on his cheek.

By the time she entered her own room, opened the connecting doors and used the bathroom, Greg was sound asleep. She could hear the rhythmic sound of his breathing. McKella slid beneath the covers of her own bed, and realized she wanted to make love with Greg. Their attraction might be simple proximity, or maybe the adrenaline rush from all the excitement. Whatever the reason, she still wanted to make love with him.

Could she do that one time and walk away unscathed?

I plan to die a bachelor, you know.

She believed him. He wasn't going to offer marriage. And he was still keeping secrets. Yet, he wanted children. She'd heard the wistful tone in his voice.

They were a lot alike, she suspected.

GREG WOKE TO A DRIVING THIRST, a raging headache and pain throughout most of his body. For just a moment, he thought he was a teenager again, alone in the hospital and more scared than he'd ever been in his life. Images from the scene of the car crash whirled through his mind. He blinked around at the dim hospital room. But there were drapes on these windows and the scent lingering in his nostrils was womanly rather than antiseptic.

And the heat stirring his loins this morning was due to the woman in the room next door.

McKella.

Cautiously, he disentangled himself from the sheets, cringing at the pain. No wonder he'd awakened dreaming about the accident. He hadn't hurt this badly since that fateful night. He made it to the bathroom, and the face that stared back at him from the mirror was not a reassuring sight. He looked like a drunk after a three-day bender. He hadn't even managed to get out of his clothing last night.

He walked through the connecting door to the next room and peered at the woman in the bed. Her hair tumbled about her face, and she looked so young and peaceful in sleep. Trusting.

Greg returned to his own room, closing the connecting doors as quietly as he could. The clock next to the bed read two minutes after three. He'd slept for more than twelve hours.

Greg flipped through the directory of services on the desk next to the telephone and lifted the receiver. If the woman on the other end was surprised by his list of requests, she didn't say so. She promised to see what she could do. Greg hung up, struggling to get free of his clothing and the sling so that he could shower.

Twenty minutes later, there was a knock at the main door.

He was thankful that the delivery person was male. He wrapped the towel awkwardly around his middle, and invited the man and his packages inside.

Greg signed the bill and added a generous tip. The razor was a disposable, but he didn't care. Removing the stubble from his face felt wonderful. The shop hadn't carried underwear, but no one would know what he wore or didn't wear beneath a pair of sweatpants. Getting the extra-large T-shirt on, one handed, took a bit of effort, and the results were dorky looking, he decided, but there was no help for it. McKella would have to assist him in rebinding the shoulder.

The dressing on his leg was wet and uncomfortable, too. McKella was not going to be happy. He was supposed to keep the wound dry, but getting clean had taken precedence. McKella would probably scold him, but he didn't mind. Her scolding showed that she cared.

Whoa. Where was he going with that thought? No place he could afford to go, that was for sure. He reached for the connecting door, and found her on the other side looking rumpled and angry and wonderfully adorable. Her hair hung in unkept lanks and her clothing was impossibly wrinkled—but she would always look beautiful to him.

"Do you know what time it is?"

"Four o'clock?" he hazarded.

"Four-ten. Where did you get those clothes and why didn't you wake me?"

"Good morning to you, too."

"Afternoon," she corrected fiercely.

He captured her lips and kissed her before she even

realized what he intended. She drew back looking startled.

"You taste like mint." Her tone was accusing.

"Toothpaste."

"You have toothpaste?" Amber eyes glowed.

"And two toothbrushes. I even have clothes for you."

She pushed past him into the room.

"Why don't you take a shower and I'll order us some food from room service. Hungry?"

She lifted a pale-pink T-shirt from the bag on the bed. Louisville Slugger was printed demurely above the pocket. He thought the sentiment appropriate in her case. The sweatpants were in a matching pink.

Greg shrugged. "I just gave them sizes. We'll have to go shopping," he explained, "but at least we can go out in public without causing a riot. The gift shop didn't offer a lot of choices. No underwear, I'm afraid, but they did have lipstick and a hairbrush."

She held the T-shirt against her chest and stared at him. He couldn't tell what she was thinking, but what *he* was thinking would probably earn him a slap.

"You untaped your arm. Did you get your bandages wet?"

"Uh—"

"I'll change them as soon as I shower. Are you feeling okay?"

He stepped toward her, but she backed away, warding him off with the bag holding the T-shirt. "Don't you even think about kissing me again. Haven't you ever heard of morning breath?"

"It's afternoon," he reminded her with a grin. "Besides, you couldn't taste bad if you tried."

She tilted her head to one side. "I thought you said I couldn't *look* bad if I tried."

"That, too," he agreed. "Now stop fishing for compliments and go take your shower."

"I intend to."

She returned to her room, leaving the connecting door open. He heard the snick of the bathroom lock and grinned. A short time after the shower stopped, he heard her muttering.

"What's wrong?" he called out.

The door opened and she poked her head outside. A halo of steam surrounded her. Her hair was wrapped in a towel and her cheeks were flushed. She looked gorgeous.

"I can't wear this shirt," she told him.

"Wrong size? Let me see."

"Not a chance."

Intrigued, he stepped over to the door. "How bad can it be?"

"I am not leaving this bathroom dressed like this."

"Too small?"

"Yes. No."

She glared at him, and he spread his hands. "I can't fix it if you won't tell me what's wrong."

"They must have something besides T-shirts."

"Sweatshirts."

"Fine. I'll take one."

"It's too hot outside for a sweatshirt."

"I don't care."

"McKella, let me see."

"No."

Greg leaned his weight against the door and she stepped back quickly.

The pink T-shirt hugged her body, emphasizing each

curve. And the two curves it hugged the best captivated his stare.

Greg cleared his throat. "You're right, you can't wear that in public."

"I look like a twenty-dollar hooker."

He shook his head. "Thousands wouldn't be enough."

Her blush started well below the collar of her T-shirt and extended up to the white bath towel on her head.

Desire filled him. "That T-shirt is almost as sexy as the gold bathing suit."

Her blush ignited, painting her face a brilliant red. Surprise and longing seemed to gaze back at him from her amber eyes. She quivered when he reached out to trace a path down her cheek. God, he liked touching her.

"Is your skin this soft everywhere, McKella?"

She swallowed hard. The towel slid down her forehead. Greg unwrapped the terrycloth before she could stop him, and her hair tumbled in damp strands around her face and neck.

"It's wet," she protested.

"Uh-huh. Smells good, too." He drew her closer, spanning her spine with the flat of his hand, wishing he had both hands to use on her. Her eyes grew heavy-lidded in anticipation.

"Do you want me to kiss you?" he asked.

"Yes."

"Thank God."

His lips covered hers, swallowing her moan of pleasure. Her hands reached up to encircle his neck as he cupped the back of her head to draw her closer. He traced her lips with his tongue, watching her eyes darken in passion and flutter closed. She clung to him, parting her lips, and he delved inside her mouth.

Her body nestled against him. A perfect, tight fit. Tension built as her hands stroked his shoulders and back with fevered movements. He brought his own hand around to cup her tempting breast beneath the soft cotton. She moaned and bit his tongue lightly, setting him on fire.

Her nipple hardened between his fingers. He drew his lips from her mouth and traced a path down her neck, loving the small sounds of pleasure she made. He thrust against her, pinning her to the wall, wanting her with a passion that negated everything else. She lifted her face…

Someone rapped on the outside door to Greg's room. ''Damn!''

McKella looked bereft as he turned and strode through the connecting doorway to his room.

The boy from room service beamed at him, then trollied the heavily laden cart into the room. The scent of coffee wafted through the air. Greg heard the connecting door close. He signed the bill and tipped the youth instead of surrendering to the urge to ring the fellow's neck. After the youth left, Greg rapped on McKella's door.

''Come and eat while the food's hot.''

She opened the door, rubbing the long strands of her damp hair with a towel. Her lips were puffy from his kisses and they quivered slightly as he stared at her. She draped the bath towel around her neck so it hung off her shoulders to cover her breasts.

''Eat first,'' he told her gruffly. ''I know you'll want to get back to the hospital.''

She followed him to the table.

"I already called the hospital," she said. "Dad hasn't regained consciousness, but he's definitely showing signs of coming around. The nurse said it could happen any time now."

Greg relaxed. "We'll head over there as soon as we finish—"

Her eyes swung up to meet his.

"—eating," he added.

She blushed and looked down at the tray. "We already missed the afternoon session. We can't get in now until seven." She reached for a fruit cup and lifted a spoon.

"So we have three hours to kill."

"I need to go shopping, and we need to pick up my uncle's car, and—"

"McKella."

She raised her head, quickly swallowing a bite of melon. As skittish as a virgin on her wedding night, Greg thought—without humor.

"You don't have to worry that I'll jump your bones..."

"I was afraid of that," she said. "You're going to make *me* do all the work."

Chapter Ten

McKella raised a forkful of the Spanish omelette, chewed and swallowed, all the while trying to pretend she wasn't nervous enough to jump out of her skin.

"You want to explain that remark?" Greg asked quietly.

"No. Not particularly."

"McKella, I'm not the marrying sort."

"So you said. I believe I have a problem along those lines myself. You'd better eat. It's getting cold." She forked in another mouthful of food without tasting anything. Her nerves pulsed with tension.

"Teasing me isn't a good idea at the moment," he warned. "I want you too much."

"Well, that's reassuring. I'd hate to have to seduce an unwilling man. Eat."

She felt his eyes on her as she swallowed, but didn't lift her head to meet his gaze. This was much harder than she'd expected. She'd never before wanted to seduce a man.

His fork settled against the plate with a clatter. "Look at me and say that."

"Say what?" She set her own fork down without a sound and raised her eyes to his. A mistake, she realized at once. Blue-green eyes glittered like gems. Her blood raced at the sensual expression on his expressive face.

"Are you planning to seduce me?" he asked very softly.

"Yes."

"What about your wedding vows?"

"My marriage will be annulled, Greg, whether Paul is a bigamist or not." Without looking away she reached into her fruit cup, selected a small bite of cantaloupe with two fingers, and raised it to her lips. She was surprised she didn't drop the dripping slice of fruit. She bit down on the melon, nervous that she might ruin everything by choking.

His eyes flashed, following her motions with a hunger that sent impulses skittering to every part of her body.

A leashed tension pulsed across the table. Never had she felt so wanted by a man. The knowledge was almost euphoric. Emboldened by his desire, she smiled and followed his downward gaze to where the towel covered her jutting breasts.

Slowly, she drew the damp cloth from her shoulders, dropping it with careless deliberation to the floor behind her chair. Her breasts seemed to swell, the nipples pushing against the cotton fabric of her shirt.

"You're doing a hell of a job," he told her.

"Good. I was going to start with whipped cream, but the waiter seems to have forgotten to leave us any."

His startled expression gave way to a deep-throated chuckle that rippled across her skin. "Whipped cream?" he repeated. His eyebrows arched in amusement.

"I'm not certain exactly what I'd do with the topping, you understand, but I feel certain you'd have a few suggestions."

He stared pointedly at her chest before returning her smile wickedly. "Yeah. I would."

"Thought so." Feeling braver and more confident every second, she leaned forward and extended the other half of the melon to him between her fingers. "Want a bite?"

He had to steady her wrist, her hand shook so badly. Then his lips closed over her thumb and forefinger, and she thought he might have to steady all of her. The heat of his mouth captured her finger and he sucked, drawing a wave of intense longing through her.

"C'mere," he whispered.

Rising on legs of gelatin, she took the two steps that brought her within range of his hard masculine body.

He drew her closer, his gaze intense. "You have another fruit I want to taste."

He traced a circle around her aching nipples, plucking first one and then the other, bringing a soft gasp to her lips. Before she could pull back from the incredible sensation, he closed his mouth over her nearest breast, shirt and all. McKella reached for his shoulders as her legs began to buckle.

Greg inserted his knee between them, and suddenly she was sitting astride his good leg, feeling the incredible pressure of his thigh against her aching need.

"I don't think we'll need the whipped cream, this time," he told her as his hand continued to massage her.

"No. I..." Her words got lost in her moan of pleasure as he slid his hand under her shirt and cupped her bared skin. The touch was electric.

Their lips fused as she sought to taste him. She held his face in both hands, nibbling at his lips and chin, then placing butterfly kisses along the strong column of his throat. She licked at the erratic pulse that beat there, matching the cadence of her own.

"McKella, we need to slow down." He breathed the words against her ear before his lips captured the earlobe and began to suck lightly.

She moaned again, her hands drifting downward. "You've got it wrong. We need to hurry."

"McKella!"

She found him beneath the elastic waistband, hard and waiting. Her fingers caressed him, measuring him, teasing him freely.

"You're playing with fire."

"Lightning," she corrected. "White-hot lightning."

Somehow they made it to the bed. McKella was surprised when he lay back, letting her take the lead.

"This is *your* seduction, I believe."

"So it is."

He cooperated as she removed his sweatpants. She tried to calm the wash of feelings that rushed through her when she saw him hard and naked before her.

"McKella? I know the scars are pretty bad—" he began.

"What scars?" But then she looked further, saw more proof of the crash he had mentioned before, and laid her lips along his thigh and the worst of his scarring, careful of the bandage marking his newest addition.

"They must have hurt."

"Once. A long time ago."

She returned her lips to their task, drawing nearer to the junction of his thighs.

He stilled her by placing his unstrapped hand along her shoulder. "No more. Not this time or I won't last. Take off your clothes. I want to see all of you."

He looked at her with such longing that she didn't hesitate. She drew off the damp shirt and sweatpants.

His avid expression added to her sense of womanly power. Then he touched her with sure, swift, certain movements that made her squirm with pleasure. Unable to stand his teasing, she moved to straddle his yearning body.

"Yes. Please, 'Kella."

She lowered herself slowly onto the probing hardness of his shaft. Immediately, she felt stretched and taken by him even though she was the one doing the taking. This was a heady, thrilling sensation unlike anything she'd ever known. Hot lightning, indeed, fusing them together the way a man and woman were meant to be. Then all thoughts disappeared beneath the incredible act of loving Greg and being loved in return.

GREG CUDDLED MCKELLA against his body. No woman had ever made love to him with such delightful, untutored abandon. How was he ever going to walk away from her now?

He loved her. Against all reason, against all common sense, he loved her. But could he ever tell her?

The question lay bitter in his mind.

"Oh, no, look at the time," she said abruptly. "Greg, let me up. We have to do something about my blouse. I can't wear that T-shirt to the hospital."

"I happen to have very fond memories of that T-shirt," he teased. "But you're right. You can't wear it in front of anyone but me. Let me throw on some clothes and run downstairs. Give me your bra size and

I'll see what I can find.'' Blushing, she told him, and
he left her worrying about her damp hair and looking
for a hair dryer.

There were several shops within walking distance,
he discovered, including a woman's specialty store.
Shopping for McKella was a unique and strangely satisfying thing to do. The lacy display of bras and panties
didn't fluster him a bit. He did bypass the white ones
in favor of two skin-colored scraps of material, and
when he would have reached for a casual top he was
sure would work with the sweatpants, his gaze was
caught by a skirt-and-blouse outfit on a nearby man-
nequin.

"Can I help you, sir?"

He smiled at the clerk who'd approached him.
"Yes."

Shoes were a bit more tricky, but a pair of open
sandals solved the problem nicely. Despite the fact that
the number of packages was now reaching the awk-
ward stage, he stopped by a men's store and grabbed
a change of clothing for himself as well.

He really needed his left arm. McKella would just
have to help him unstrap the thing. He knew from experience that immobilizing the arm and shoulder would
help it heal faster, but it wasn't essential.

Holding McKella in both arms was far more important.

With that in mind, he hurried back to the hotel. He
had to set the packages down to get the door open.
McKella sat on the side of the bed, holding the telephone in her hand. Her hair was loose and soft around
her face the way he liked it, but her expression sent
talons of fear piercing through his gut.

''What's wrong?'' he demanded. He strode forward. ''Who was on the phone?''

She tried to laugh but the sound came out brittle. ''When I answered, the person hung up.''

The talons flexed in reaction to her words.

''It was probably a wrong number, Greg.''

''Not a chance. Hurry and change, we're getting out of here.''

Her hands reached for the bag. Greg expected her to go all shy on him and take the bag into the bathroom, but once again, she didn't do the expected. Her pleasure at the sight of the brightly colored outfit was genuine.

''It's beautiful.''

Satisfied, he smiled. ''Will everything fit?''

''I think so.''

Greg watched with unabashed interest as she dropped her pants and stepped into the bikini panties he'd selected. They reminded him of the gold bathing suit, nearly disappearing against her skin. While her actions were brisk rather than seductive, Greg found himself wanting her again. Only the color in her cheeks told him that she was aware of him watching—aware and just the smallest bit uncertain. This sort of intimacy was obviously new to her. She didn't have a coy bone in her body.

He forced himself to reach for his own bag. He struggled out of the T-shirt, replacing it with a more dressy sports shirt. He was still grappling with the light blue twill pants when McKella's hands were there, helping him.

Her fingers on the button at his waist were almost his undoing. ''If you keep touching me, we're getting right back into that bed.''

Her hand stilled and she stepped back. "If I didn't have to get to the hospital by seven, I'd take you up on that boast."

"Boast?"

She laughed, then twirled for his inspection. "What do you think?"

"I think we need to get our clothes back off."

"Later." Her smile was filled with promise. "Are these shoes for me?"

He let himself be diverted, knowing they didn't have time for what he wanted to do, and relieved that she still wanted him and wasn't having regrets.

She tried on the sandals dubiously. "A bit big," she said, "but they'll stay on my feet—and they certainly go better with this outfit than the shoes I was wearing. What do you think?"

He said what was in his heart. "I think you're exquisite."

She looked away quickly, her gaze fastening on the last bag. "Want some help with your new shoes?" she asked.

He lifted a pair of loafers from the box and dropped them on the floor so he could slide his feet inside.

"Smart thinking," she approved.

"Thank you. Shall we go?" He was anxious to leave the hotel. If McKella's husband was trying to locate her, she needed to be out of harm's way.

At the hospital, after seeing her disappear inside the relative security of the ICU, Greg went downstairs to look in on her private investigator. Eric Henning was sitting up reading a western.

"What happened to you?" he asked as soon as he spotted Greg in the doorway.

"McConnel," Greg answered.

"Didn't I tell you to watch out for that knife?"

Greg grinned. "This time he had a gun."

Henning swore. "McKella?"

"Upstairs visiting her father. She's bruised and scared, but otherwise unharmed. McConnel got away with the process her people were developing."

Henning muttered a more creative obscenity.

"Yeah," Greg agreed. "How are you doing?"

"Fever's gone. I'll be out of here tomorrow. A friend of mine's been doing some digging on McConnel for me. It appears he reverts to his real name until he's ready to move on to his next target."

"So if I go hunting for Jason McConnel instead of Paul Dinsmore, I might find him?"

Henning shook his head. "I gave this info to the cops this morning. They're already looking."

"I wish to hell they'd find him. Someone called McKella's hotel room today, but no one knew where we were staying."

Henning shook his head. "Why would her husband do that if he already has the process? I'd expect him to sell the info as quick as he could and get out."

Greg stared at the other man thoughtfully. "Yeah."

"I've been thinking about that plane the cops said flew into Bermuda. It occurs to me the pilot might have nothing to do with Jason McConnel and everything to do with Paul Dinsmore."

Greg saw what Henning was getting at. "A hit man?"

"Those people never forget. Thanks to Betty Jane, Dinsmore's name was being splashed everywhere. Maybe someone went to check out Paul Dinsmore."

"And found Betty Jane instead?"

Henning nodded. "Anything's possible."

"If that was the case, they wouldn't go after Mc-Kella."

"No, but they wouldn't hesitate to take out anyone who got in their way, either."

True enough, and it might be the reason Betty Jane was killed.

Greg was thinking along different lines. "Can you run another check—this time on her uncle?"

Henning raised an eyebrow. "The cops are already looking at him. They say he's a pilot. What do you think I might find?"

"A lack of money. In the event of her death, Patterson reverts to the uncle, not McKella's husband. I want to cover all the bases."

"I'll get right on it. Meanwhile, see if you can keep McKella safe."

Greg frowned. "That's my plan."

He didn't like Henning's predatory ways where McKella was concerned, but Greg comforted himself with the thought that she had given herself to him. He left the detective reaching for a telephone, and headed back upstairs.

McKella strode through the double doors of the unit a few minutes later, looking more at ease than she had in a long while.

"Is he conscious?" Greg asked.

"No, but I'm sure he could hear me." She smiled. "The nurse says it's only a matter of time. His vitals are strong. Even the oncologist is pleased."

"I'm glad." He slid his arm around her shoulders. Holding her was becoming a nice habit. "McKella, would you like me to take a look at your books?"

"Do you think Paul tampered with something? Uncle Larry will find any discrepancies."

When he didn't say anything, sudden comprehension lit her expression. "You're back to not trusting my uncle."

"I don't trust anyone except you. Your uncle inherits the company if something happens to you."

"Uncle Larry wouldn't hurt me. Besides, he sold Dad his share of the company years ago."

"Uh-huh. When he had a reversal of fortune and needed money in a hurry. Are you seeing a pattern here? Next time that happens, your dad gives him a job. But it's a job, not joint ownership. His finances slip again and the results are a little embezzlement. He lives high, McKella. Expensive car and I'll bet he has an expensive house. I saw his office, remember? A lot fancier than yours."

"Greg, that isn't fair. I told you he has no one else to spend the money on besides himself." But her protest was weaker now. She was thinking, instead of instinctively protecting her relative.

"Uh-huh. But what if he's having another problem? Patterson is being run by some outsider who happened to marry the owner's daughter."

"You make Uncle Larry sound like a monster."

"Maybe he is." He held up his hand to forestall her next protest. "And maybe I'm seeing shadows on the wall. All I'm suggesting is we take a look and find out."

McKella frowned. "Let's go."

McKELLA RUBBED THE BACK of her neck. They'd been poring over the files in her uncle's office for hours now, and Greg had to admit he hadn't found a thing wrong.

Loyalty to her uncle made her glad, but honesty made her confront the truth of Greg's words.

"What's wrong?" he asked, looking up and trying to rub his bad leg without bothering the sutures. "Did you find something?"

"No, and I don't expect to, but I've been thinking..."

"Uh-oh."

She made a face, but her thoughts were too troubling to keep inside any longer.

"Everyone believes Paul killed Betty Jane and Eleanor. We know he stole the research on Ben's new process and probably stabbed Eric Henning to prevent him from telling me about his phoney past."

"But?" Greg prodded, standing to work the cramps out of his leg.

"But...he didn't kill us when he had the chance, Greg. And Constable Freer thinks there's significance to that private plane that flew into Bermuda."

"Apart from the timing and the fact that it was stolen and the pilot used phoney ID, why would he think there is significance to that plane?"

McKella grimaced. "You sure have a way of making a question sound like an indictable offense."

He smiled, a slow sexy smile that erased the fatigue and pain lines around his eyes and mouth. Her breath lodged in her throat as he came around the desk to stand beside her chair.

"We should get another hotel room," he said softly.

Her heart thundered at his look. "Why?"

"You know why." He had to reach past his immobile left arm to caress her face. McKella trembled at the touch of his fingers on her skin.

"Are we done looking for shadows?"

"No, but it will take time to do a detailed audit."

McKella set down her stack of papers and stood. "Face it, Greg. We're wasting time."

Greg rubbed his jaw. "You may be right."

"Of course I'm right."

Greg suddenly yawned and went to perch on the edge of the desk. In the process, he dislodged Larry's in-basket. Papers scattered to the floor.

"Sorry."

McKella hurried forward. "We're too tired to be doing this," she scolded. "I'll put these back and…" She stopped moving, her eyes scanning the paper, her mind absorbing the words like blows.

"What's that?" he asked.

She handed him the paper, trying to ignore the cold hollowness inside her.

"NewEyes?" he asked, reading the logo at the top.

"They're our chief competitors."

She watched him skim the document. Three weeks ago, NewEyes had offered to buy Patterson Opticals. The lucrative proposal in her hands had been made to Larry Patterson. The document referred to previous discussions on the subject.

"It's a lot of money," she said sadly.

"Your uncle obviously gave them reason to think he is or will be the new owner."

She shivered. "A mistake?"

"Three weeks old? Somehow, I think it's a stretch even for you to assume good old Uncle Larry conveniently forgot to mention he's been having discussions of this sort."

McKella closed her eyes. "Yes."

"I admire your loyalty, but it's time to take the blinders off. If you die, Larry inherits. Accepting this offer would make him a wealthy man."

Her eyes sprang open. "We should go and talk to him."

"We'll let the police go and talk to him."

"He's my uncle."

"Who has reason to want you dead."

"I won't believe that."

But she did.

"You know, it never seemed odd that Uncle Larry seldom did things with Dad and me," she said thoughtfully. "Uncle Larry was always spending holidays in Europe or Aspen or any number of places. He and Dad always had different lifestyles."

And if recently he'd started to buck her at board meetings, well, she'd thought he was trying to take her father's place as a mentor. She'd been wise enough to listen, but strong enough to make her own decisions—even when some of those decisions made her uncle angry.

"But why kill Paul's wives?" she asked.

"Maybe he didn't. We could be dealing with two different situations here."

"Thanks a lot. You mean two men want me dead?"

She leaned against his good shoulder, welcoming the comfort. Greg was solid and dependable—a shield against the horrible thoughts hammering at her mind.

"Let's call it a night, 'Kella. We'll take your uncle's car and find a motel."

"Not the place we stayed last night?"

Greg shook his head. "Not after that phone call. I don't want anyone even guessing where we are tonight. In the morning, we'll go to the police."

"Maybe."

He eyed her sharply. "We'll argue the point later."

Greg put the offer in a manila envelope, and they

closed the office and headed downstairs. Ralph wasn't at his desk. A bag of chocolate chip cookies and a bottle of soda attested to the fact that he couldn't be far away.

Greg studied the parking lot while McKella signed them out.

Ralph's truck and her uncle's car were the only two vehicles in sight. Greg was right, she decided. The parking lot was much too dark at night. As soon as she went back to work she'd make some changes—starting with a call to that security firm he'd recommended.

They were almost at the car when Greg suddenly pulled on her arm, bringing her up short. "Go back inside."

"What's wrong?" Tomorrow, she swore, she'd get another pair of contacts. She was tired of seeing things in the distance as one big blur.

"Something's sticking out of the trunk of the car. Call the police." He handed her the manila envelope and gave her a slight shove in the direction of the building.

The stubborn man just loved to play hero. "We're already out in the open, Greg. He could have shot us by now if that was his intention."

Greg cursed, never taking his eyes from the vehicle. The only movement was some distant traffic on the street beyond the fence.

"Will you at least stay here?" He didn't wait for her answer. He moved forward, limping slightly.

He reached the trunk and fingered the dark scrap of cloth. McKella would never have even noticed it. Slowly, he inserted the key. The trunk popped open.

McKella hadn't even realized she'd followed Greg, but now she stood to one side as the trunk light bathed the interior in a muted yellow glow. Something lay crumpled inside. McKella walked closer as Greg lifted a man's head by the back of his hair.

"Greg?"

"McKella, get back!"

But it was too late. She'd seen enough. The man she had known as Paul Dinsmore was dead. A single gunshot wound to the temple.

She gagged and turned away, horrified.

"He's been dead a while, McKella. Probably since last night. The stuff he took is under the body."

"But who—?"

"It looks like a professional hit to me."

"But he wasn't really Paul Dinsmore."

"I know. But maybe *they* didn't. Or maybe they just wanted to send a message to anyone using that name."

Greg closed the trunk and led her inside. He headed for the information desk in search of the telephone, while McKella stared blankly around the empty lobby. Her gaze locked on the pair of dark shoes protruding from behind the planter along the far wall.

"Greg—" Her voice cracked and broke.

"This phone line's been cut," he told her.

"Greg!" She moved forward, terrified of what she'd find, but unable to stop herself. Ralph was a family man, so proud of his ten-year-old son and nine-year-old daughter. If he was dead…if it was her fault…

She heard Greg come after her. Somehow, she wasn't surprised when he reached Ralph before she did. Blood trickled down the older man's face from a cut near his temple.

"Is he—?"

"No. He's still breathing. Come on."

He practically dragged her to the bank of elevators.

"What are you doing?"

"Getting you upstairs where we might be safe."

Horror gripped her. "You think the killer is still here?"

"Someone is."

They rode to the second floor in silence. Greg checked the hall before he let her step out of the elevator. He hit the hold button to keep the doors open and locked on their floor, then, quietly, motioned for her to follow.

They made little noise going past the row of closed offices. Greg entered hers, looked around and motioned her inside. "Keep the lights off," he whispered, closing the door without a sound.

"Greg, if the killer is here, he heard the elevator."

"But he won't know for sure where we are unless we make noise." He reached for her telephone, obviously relieved when the line lit up.

"Unless he's in a connecting office. Then he'll see the light," she pointed out.

"That's a chance we'll have to take. This is Greg Wyman," he said into the mouthpiece. "I'm at Patterson Opticals with McKella Patterson. We've got a dead body in a car outside and the night watchman is injured and unconscious in the downstairs lobby. We've reason to believe someone is inside the building."

McKella listened to his low voice, and tried to stop shaking.

"No, ma'am. I can't do that. I've got to go back downstairs to open the gates so the officers can get inside the lot."

McKella hadn't thought about that. The police couldn't get in unless they overrode the security system. Greg hung up as she turned and started for the door.

"Where do you think you're going?" he demanded.

"To release—"

"You'll stay right here."

"No, I won't. I know where the circuits are and it's my company."

"And the killer wants you dead, McKella."

"Who turned you invincible?"

They both heard a distinct thump. The muffled sound came from somewhere down the hall.

"Wait here," he ordered. "This time I *mean* it."

"Don't go out there." She clung to his good arm, blocking his path to the door. "Don't you watch horror movies?"

He made a soft sound, then she felt his lips against her hair. "I love you, McKella."

I'm the man who's falling in love with you.

God, how she loved this man. "Your timing stinks."

He chuckled. "I still have to take down the system so the police can get inside," he whispered.

"We'll both go."

"No." His tension communicated itself, as did his determination. "It isn't safe."

"Why didn't we take care of that when we were downstairs?"

"Because we didn't think of it. Go hide under the desk."

"I'm not hiding under a desk, Greg. I'm going with you. We'll be safer together."

Greg hesitated. Exasperated, he nodded. "All right, but let me scout the hall first. We'll take the stairs."

McKella nodded. As Greg disappeared, she peered around her office for a weapon. He was in no condition to face a killer unarmed. Especially not a professional killer.

She moved around the desk and heard a muffled thud. Fear paralyzed her. A door slammed shut.

"Greg?" Silence blanketed the building, wrapping her in a cocoon of fear.

She peered into the gloomy hall. The reception area at the end of the corridor was filled with long gray shadows. Only a lackluster light trickled in through the windows at that end. Nothing moved.

Her gaze skimmed the line of doors, all firmly shut. If Greg was okay, he would have answered her. So he wasn't okay. He needed help. The gold-plated letter opener fit neatly into her hand.

Shaking, McKella slipped out of her sandals and headed into the hall. She eyed the elevator, gaping open in silent, dark invitation. Fear sent quivers racing down her back. She strained to hear something. Anything. The sense of waiting danger enveloped her like a malevolent lover, stroking her nerves to fevered pitch.

She stepped forward as quietly as she could. Where was Greg? He had to be behind one of these doors, but which one? The opening for the staircase across from the elevator beckoned. McKella shook her head, remembering all too clearly her last adventure in a stairwell.

One careful step after another, she inched forward. At Paul's door, she paused. Fear obstructed her throat. Her heart beat too loudly for her to hear anything on the other side of the wooden door—even if there was something to hear. Now nearly running, she headed for the open elevator. The only way to help Greg was to let the police inside the grounds.

She did run the last few feet, blood pulsing through her veins, making her ears ring with silent pressure. She darted inside, hand reaching for the lobby button even as she turned.

And a dark figure moved out of the deep corner shadow.

McKella screamed as black-gloved hands reached for her throat. Fingers settled, choking off her oxygen. She had only a second to realize that the assailant was dressed completely in black, even to the hood covering hair and face. Then the elevator doors slid closed and the floor lurched gently as they started to descend.

She couldn't breathe.

She was going to die.

With fading strength, she raised the letter opener, aiming for the vulnerable side of the assailant's neck. The blade plunged through the hood, into his flesh. He yelped in surprise and pain.

Her neck was suddenly free. McKella raised her knee with every bit of muscle left in her. He screamed as she found her target, but his backhanded blow sent her reeling against the far wall of the elevator.

She was aware of the elevator lurching to a stop. Hands fumbled, reaching again for her throat. She lowered her chin, trying to deflect them. With her fists, she beat at the black shape. Through a long dark tunnel, she saw the doors open at his back. Heard a shout.

Suddenly the hands released her. McKella slid to the floor, sucking greedily at the vital air. Dimly, she was aware of yells and a scuffle, but she couldn't seem to open her eyes. She concentrated on breathing in and out.

Someone hunkered at her side. "You will need to call an ambulance."

She knew that formal voice. Constable Freer. She lifted heavy eyelids to see his concerned face swim into view.

"Greg!" Her intended shout came out as an unintelligible whisper of sound that strained her throat.

"Do not try to speak, McKella," Freer cautioned.

But she had to speak. She had to tell him about Greg. Greg must be hurt. He might be dying.

Someone shouldered his way to stand over her, and Freer stepped aside. Greg sat beside her, pulling her against his body. Blood ran down the side of his face.

"You...look...awful," she forced out. Her throat hurt too much for more, but her relief was nearly overwhelming. He was all right. Greg was alive.

"Don't try to talk. Don't move. You'll be okay now." He raised his eyes to the faces above them. "Where's the ambulance?"

"Easy, Wyman. It's on the way." She recognized Lieutenant Stone's voice, though she couldn't see him. "How bad are you hurt?" he asked Greg.

"Mostly my pride. He clobbered me as I passed an office. The pain stunned me long enough for him to get to McKella. How did you guys get inside?"

"We were already en route when your call came in. The night watchman called about a break-in. He deactivated the gate before he was attacked."

Two uniformed policeman held the black-garbed figure between them. One ripped the hood from his head. Larry Patterson raised his eyes to look straight into McKella's. "It was nothing personal," he told her.

Greg started to rise, but McKella gripped his arm. Greg allowed her to pull him back to her side, and settled for a string of curses aimed at the older Patterson.

"I had no choice," Larry said calmly. "My brother turned the company over to her instead of me." His blue eyes were chilling, totally devoid of remorse.

"She did nothing to earn the ownership," he explained, "while I helped *build* Patterson Opticals. If she had simply drunk the wine I doctored at the reception, all of this might have been avoided. Her husband would have taken the blame when she lapsed into a coma and died. I knew all about his past, of course. It was so ironic the way I kept stumbling over his wives. McKella should have died at the café that day. You've been a serious nuisance," he told Greg.

McKella was sure that if his hands hadn't been in restraints, her uncle would have reached up to flick off a bit of imaginary lint. Greg uttered a low string of profanities, but her grip kept him in place at her side.

"You returned my call," she whispered. "The message in Bermuda…"

"A cell phone," he explained, unperturbed.

Stone turned to one of the officers. "Tell me you read him his rights," he pleaded.

"Yes, sir, I sure did."

McKella tried to swallow. Greg saw her distress. "Where's that ambulance? I can practically see her throat swelling."

"They're pulling up right now, Mr. Wyman."

"Her father regained consciousness several hours ago," Freer stated. "He told quite a tale of betrayal."

"You want to talk betrayal," Larry said. "My brother knew I needed money, but he turned the company over to his daughter rather than sell it and split the proceeds. The fire was an accident, of course, but fortuitous. I thought it would surely finish him off."

McKella stared in horror.

"Mr. Patterson is pressing charges for attempted murder," Stone said.

Larry frowned. "Meddling fool." He paused to survey the people looking at him. "I believe I'd like to call a lawyer now," he stated.

McKella closed her eyes and sank back against the solid comfort of Greg's chest.

Epilogue

"Ms. Patterson? This is Eric Henning."

McKella stared at the telephone beneath her fingers, ignoring the sense of déjà vu.

"Look, I know you didn't ask for this, but I've been doing a little digging over the past few months, and I think you ought to know, Greg Wyman may not be who he says he is."

McKella looked down at the man sleeping so peacefully in her rumpled bed—rumpled from hours of glorious, perfect lovemaking.

"In fact, I have reason to believe he's really Brendon Gregory McConnel."

Her heart softened as her eyes traced the tiny lines beneath Greg's chin. You had to look closely to spot the plastic surgery. Someone had done a wonderful job fifteen years ago.

"According to the police report, Paul Dinsmore had a second man asleep in the back seat of his car. I think that other guy was BG McConnel, who changed his name to Wyman."

Yes, she was sure of it as well.

"There's no question Dinsmore was killed. The car belonged to him, but the passenger didn't have any ID.

That's where some of the confusion came in that night. One thing's sure, I can't find any record of a Greg Wyman before that time. Let me know if you want me to follow up on this. Or I'd be happy to have a talk with your Mr. Wyman.''

McKella smiled. How odd to have so many champions.

She contemplated Greg's sleeping form. Why hadn't he deleted the message? He had listened to their voice mail when they came in last night, but he had said only that she had a message. And at that point, messages were the last thing on her mind. Although, they never had gotten around to trying the whipped cream.

Maybe later.

In the past five months, her life had undergone drastic changes. Uncle Larry was still awaiting trial for the murder of Eleanor Beauchamp. He wasn't talking anymore, but the police were pretty certain he wasn't responsible for Paul's murder. They believed Paul had been followed to the plant, then executed with the gun he'd taken from her uncle's safe, probably while Ralph was making his rounds elsewhere inside the building. After all these years, someone had finally collected on the contract on Paul Dinsmore.

Once they knew where to look, they found evidence proving Larry had stolen the plane flown into Bermuda. Fingerprints tied him to the plane, and he'd all but admitted that the truck killing Eleanor Beauchamp by the café, and the incident in the hospital stairwell, had been attempts to kill McKella. But Larry was most annoyed by any suggestion that he'd killed Betty Jane as well.

Forensic evidence backed him up. The bruising pattern on Betty Jane's neck indicated a larger hand than

Larry's. Constable Freer, like Greg, believed Paul had killed Betty Jane when she'd confronted him at the cottage. Greg felt certain Paul's story of a prowler had been an attempt to divert McKella's attention.

Other evidence against Larry Patterson kept piling up. Her uncle was in heavy financial debt, and the people he had spoken to at NewEyes were more than happy to cooperate with the investigation.

McKella's father continued to recover. His cancer was in remission and the heart specialists were optimistic. He claimed that he felt terrific and planned to finally enjoy his retirement—a retirement made possible with Greg acting as CEO at Patterson Opticals.

She stifled an urge to reach out and brush back the lock of hair that had drifted over Greg's left eye. She loved him so much it was painful.

He had put his own business in his partners' hands to help her run Patterson. Her father genuinely liked Greg, though he was careful not to put his thoughts in words. Obviously, he worried that he had pushed McKella into her first marriage and was determined not to repeat that mistake.

Greg hadn't mentioned marriage since that day in the vault. She submerged any wistful thoughts along that line, thankful that he was willing to move in with her and share whatever he could of himself.

She replaced the receiver and found Greg awake and watching her. "Good morning," she said softly.

"Is it?" He propped his head on his hand.

"What's that supposed to mean?" She drew her thin robe more tightly around her body.

"You listened to Eric's message?"

"Yes."

"No questions?"

McKella saw the shadows in his light-blue eyes. She still wasn't used to seeing him without his green contacts.

"No questions," she assured him. "What do you want for breakfast? It's my turn to cook."

"McKella—"

She was already heading out the door, determined to avoid this confrontation at all costs. Their relationship was too vulnerable. Too new. She wouldn't ruin what they had with questions. The answers weren't important anymore. She knew all she needed to know about Greg Wyman. She loved him.

He caught her before she reached the stairs, uncompromisingly male and unabashedly nude. She loved him and she loved his body—every muscle, every ridge, every plane and every scar.

"I'm tired of playing games," he announced.

"Who's playing games?"

"You are. You never once asked me," he accused. "Never once."

She knew what he meant and she didn't want to have this conversation. Everything might change again, and that terrified her. She didn't want more change. She wanted Greg.

"I don't need to ask you anything," she told him with a calm she didn't feel. "You once told me you'd never lie to me."

"I never have."

"Well then?"

"Ask me," he demanded.

"It's not important."

He touched her cheek, running the back of his fingers across her skin, leaving prickles in their wake. His voice went whiskey-soft. "Yeah, McKella. It is."

"Why?"

"No more secrets. I've been waiting for you to ask me."

She glared at him, standing rigid beneath his touch. "Well, I'm not going to ask. It doesn't matter if you're Jason McConnel's brother—"

"I'm not."

The world's oxygen supply suddenly seemed depleted. "What?"

"I'm not Jason McConnel's brother. BG is dead, McKella. He died fifteen years ago driving Paul Dinsmore's car."

The room dipped and plunged as it spun. She shook her head, trying to keep the darkness at bay, trembling from head to toe. Not wanting to ask, but knowing somehow she had to get the question past her frozen lips. She pushed out one word. "How?"

"He was drunk. So was Paul. Unfortunately, so was the driver of the oncoming car." His eyes grew luminous with the intensity of his words. "He lost control of the car, somehow. They hit head-on. BG never had a chance. Paul..." He took an unsteady breath. "Paul was mangled, pinned in the wreckage. Two passersby pulled him free, terrified that the car would burst into flames."

She really didn't want to hear this, but he was right, she did have to know. Because there was only one way his words made any sense. And his pride demanded that she know the truth.

"There was no hitchhiker, was there?"

"No." He continued to watch her mercilessly.

"You're him. You're really Paul Dinsmore."

"Yes."

The room suddenly righted itself again. She drew in

a deep, satisfying breath of air. Everything made sense. He felt he couldn't marry because of the contract on his life, because anyone close to Paul Dinsmore was at risk.

A thousand questions tickled her mind, but they no longer mattered. Greg would answer them openly any time she chose to ask.

"BG was a good kid," he told her. "Bright. And so young. I was a loser with nothing to gain." Pain darkened his features. "I should have been driving that night."

"No," she protested instantly.

He smiled sadly. "He shouldn't have died, but he did. Sixteen years old. A runaway. No family besides Jason. He didn't even have identification." Greg closed his eyes in remembered distress, then opened them again.

"What he had was my wallet. He found it in his brother's room months after I left town. Then one day he saw an article in the newspaper about the warehouse shooting and trial in Frankfort. They used my name, so BG came looking for me. By then, of course, Jason had already used my identification to set up a second identity as me, but neither of us knew that."

His eyes clouded with memories of the past, and McKella ached for the visions she knew he must be recalling.

"My wallet ended up in the grass next to BG's body. Since he was driving and he fit my general description, they assumed BG was me."

"But what about dental records or fingerprints?"

"Neither of us had ever had any dental work done and, for whatever reason, they never ran his prints. Maybe they couldn't. I just don't know."

He took a deep breath. "Since no one knew BG was with me, the cops had no idea who I was. I was in no condition to tell them at first and someone had remembered seeing a hitchhiker. They assumed that's how I got in the car. By the time I could tell them different, I no longer wanted to."

She wanted to cry for his pain, but tears had deserted her.

"For weeks I lay in that hospital and wondered why I was still alive when BG was dead. I even wondered if the accident had been caused because of the price on my head. Then...I don't know...gradually it dawned on me that I was being offered a second chance. Everyone believed Paul Dinsmore was dead."

He shrugged. "I guess it sounds weird, but I felt like I owed it to BG to make something of myself. I took BG's middle name, and invented the Wyman, and told the cops what they expected to hear. Greg Wyman became a hitchhiker that Paul Dinsmore picked up that night. The rest, you know."

She wanted to hug him, to bury herself against his hard body and offer comfort, but before she could move, he turned and started back to the bedroom.

"I'm going to catch a shower," he told her without turning around. "Eggs and toast would be nice for a change. I don't think I'm up for any of that fat-free cereal this morning."

McKella watched him disappear. The longer she stood there, the angrier she became. Who did he think he was?

Had he thought she was so shallow that his identity would make a difference to her? Did he think she'd confuse him with that jerk she had married? Paul Dinsmore was dead. The newspapers had announced it in boldface—even the gangsters had to be convinced this time. There was no contract hanging over Greg's head anymore. She and Greg were the only two people alive who knew the truth—and she wasn't going to tell a soul.

So as a kid he'd walked on the wild side. Greg was a man now, and the only thing he did on the wild side these days was to make love to her.

McKella charged into the steamy bathroom and flung open the shower door. Greg blinked in surprise, then ducked his head to rinse the shampoo from his thick, dark hair.

"That's it, Wyman, I've had it." She realized her robe was getting wet and didn't care.

"Had what?"

"I'm tired of always being the one to take the first step in this relationship, but God knows, I'd wait forever if I had to wait for you. Are you going to marry me or not?"

The smile started in his eyes, but quickly spread to the corners of his lips, where it twitched to be free.

"I thought you were never planning to marry again. I thought you said—"

"I know what I said. I lied."

"I see." He was having trouble holding back that smile. He reached over and removed the wet robe from her shoulders. Instantly, her body responded to his touch.

"You don't see anything. You're a man."

The smile broke free. "So true."

She pushed her hand against his chest, holding him at bay when he would have pulled her closer. "You said we would live together until the children came."

A stillness came over him. "You're pregnant?"

"Not yet, but I'm planning to be and I'm old-fashioned. I want the ring first."

His eyes twinkled. "Hmm. You sure?"

"Of course I'm sure."

He took her robe and tossed it into the sink. "Wait here."

"What?" But she was talking to his back again.

Dripping wet, he left the bathroom. She allowed the soothing warm water to pelt her skin, afraid to hope, but wanting desperately to believe.

He returned a moment later and stepped back inside the shower stall. He reached for her finger. She stared down at the marquise diamond flanked by two brilliant rubies. He slid the ring past her knuckle. A perfect fit.

"Now can we make the baby?" he asked.

Her tears mingled with the running water. "Idiot."

"No doubt. We'll hope she gets your genes."

McKella flowed into the haven of his strong arms as the water bathed them both. "How long have you had this?"

"Since two days after Larry was arrested."

"What? Why didn't you ask me sooner?"

"I was waiting until you were sure, McKella. And you couldn't be sure until you knew the whole truth. Your dad likes me, and I can run the company. It was too much like last time."

"You're not Paul. I mean you *are*, but—"

He kissed her, drinking in her sigh of pleasure. "I know exactly what you meant," he whispered. "No more illusions. I wanted all the secrets out in the open first. And there's a condition that comes with that ring."

"A condition?" She could feel him growing hard

against her body, could feel her own quickening response.

"Uh-huh. I want us to buy a real house. One with a large yard, big enough for a swing set and maybe even a tree house. How do you feel about dogs?"

She was crying. She hated to cry. She hoped her smile didn't look as tremulous as it felt. "Dogs, plural?" she asked.

"It's negotiable. But I'd like the house. A man has to have at least one place in his life where he's the boss, even if it is in name only." He kissed her forehead.

"Are you calling me bossy?"

"Never. Hey, I'm not foolish." He fondled her nipples, bringing them to hard points.

McKella moaned softly and arched in pleasure. "I don't want to run things," she gasped, "but you should know I intend to keep my hand on every aspect of our lives."

He guided her fingers to his waiting appendage. "You can start here."

"That wasn't exactly what I meant," she told him, laughter bubbling from within. "Never mind. Maybe this is one illusion I should leave alone."

"Please don't. I think I'll go crazy if you stop."

She licked her way down his chest, satisfied when he drew in a sharp breath. "Don't worry. The world will run out of hot water long before I stop loving you."

Take 2 bestselling love stories FREE

Plus get a FREE surprise gift!

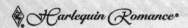

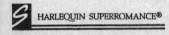

MEN at WORK

All work and no play?
Not these men!

July 1998
MACKENZIE'S LADY by Dallas Schulze

Undercover agent Mackenzie Donahue's
lazy smile and deep blue eyes were his best
weapons. But after rescuing—and kissing!—
damsel in distress Holly Reynolds, how could
he betray her by spying on her brother?

August 1998
MISS LIZ'S PASSION by Sherryl Woods

Todd Lewis could put up a building with ease,
but quailed at the sight of a classroom! Still,
Liz Gentry, his son's teacher, was no battle-ax,
and soon Todd started planning some
extracurricular activities of his own....

September 1998
A CLASSIC ENCOUNTER
by Emilie Richards

Doctor Chris Matthews was intelligent, sexy
and *very* good with his hands—which made
him all the more dangerous to single mom
Lizette St. Hilaire. So how long could she
resist Chris's special brand of TLC?

Available at your favorite retail outlet!

MEN AT WORK™

 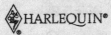

Lost & Found

All new...and filled with the mystery and romance you love!

SOMEBODY'S BABY
by Amanda Stevens in November 1998

A FATHER FOR HER BABY
by B. J. Daniels in December 1998

A FATHER'S LOVE
by Carla Cassidy in January 1999

It all begins one night when three women go into labor in the same Galveston, Texas, hospital. Shortly after the babies are born, fire erupts, and though each child and mother make it to safety, there's more than just the mystery of birth to solve now....

Don't miss this *all new* LOST & FOUND trilogy!

Available at your favorite retail outlet.

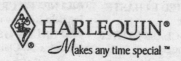

HARLEQUIN®
Makes any time special ™

Look us up on-line at: http://www.romance.net

HILF

COMING NEXT MONTH

#485 REMEMBER ME, COWBOY by Caroline Burnes
Cassidy O'Neal's world shattered the day Slate Walker lost his memory and was convicted of a crime she was sure he hadn't committed. Five years later, she'd risk her ranch and her heart to prove him innocent...but could she tell him about the daughter he never knew they had?

#486 SEND ME A HERO by Rita Herron
Her Protector
Echoing footsteps, threatening phone calls, a midnight attacker... Veronica Miller knew she was in danger, but police could find no evidence. Someone wanted her to look crazy. Could Detective Nathan Dawson save Veronica from events set in motion far in the past, on a night she couldn't remember?

#487 MYSTERY DAD by Leona Karr
Mark Richards was stunned when he came home to find his bachelor apartment occupied by two youngsters and a baby. Working with P.I. Kerri Kincaid to find the missing mother placed both Mark and Kerri in danger—and the biggest threat was to Mark's bachelor status....

#488 THE ARMS OF THE LAW by Jenna Ryan
Psychiatrist Nikita Sorensen was shaken by the hospital murders— and unsettled by officer Daniel Vachon whose bold approach to the case squared him head-to-head with Nikita. But it was soon clear the murderer aimed to draw Nikita into the web of terror. And Vachon's strong arms were the only safe harbor.

AVAILABLE THIS MONTH:

Look us up on-line at: http://www.romance.net